Jilly Cooper
Essex in 19__. Her writing career began in 1956, when she got a job as a cub reporter on the *Middlesex Independent*. Following several short stories for women's magazines, Jilly Cooper started contributing a regular column to *The Sunday Times* in 1969. She stayed with them until 1982 when she joined *The Mail on Sunday* as a bi-monthly columnist.

Her first book, *How to Stay Married*, was written in 1969. Since then she has written or helped to compile twenty-five others including six romances: *Emily*, *Bella*, *Harriet*, *Octavia*, *Prudence* and *Imogen*, and the bestselling *Riders* and *Rivals*. Her most recent non-fiction books are *Animals at War* and *The Common Years*. She has also written a television series, *It's Awfully Bad for Your Eyes, Darling*, and has often appeared as a television guest herself.

Jilly Cooper is married to publisher, Leo Cooper, and they live in the Cotswolds. They have two children, Felix and Emily, four cats and two mongrels.

Also by Jilly Cooper

RIVALS
RIDERS
EMILY
BELLA
HARRIET
OCTAVIA
IMOGEN
CLASS
SUPER COOPER
LISA & CO.

and published by Corgi Books

Jilly Cooper

Prudence

CORGI BOOKS

PRUDENCE
A CORGI BOOK 0 552 10878 2

Originally published in Great Britain by
Arlington Books Ltd.

PRINTING HISTORY
Arlington Books edition published 1978
Corgi edition published 1978
Corgi edition reprinted 1978
Corgi edition reprinted 1979 (twice)
Corgi edition reprinted 1980
Corgi edition reprinted 1983 (twice)
Corgi edition reprinted 1984 (twice)
Corgi edition reprinted 1986 (twice)
Corgi edition reprinted 1988
Corgi edition reissued 1989
Corgi edition reprinted 1989
Corgi edition reprinted 1990

Corgi Books are published by Transworld Publishers
Ltd., 61–63 Uxbridge Road, Ealing, London W5 5SA, in
Australia by Transworld Publishers (Australia) Pty. Ltd.,
15–23 Helles Avenue, Moorebank, NSW 2170, and in New
Zealand by Transworld Publishers (N.Z.) Ltd., Cnr. Moselle
and Waipareira Avenues, Henderson, Auckland.

Printed and bound in Great Britain by
Cox & Wyman Ltd., Reading, Berks.

For Maura McCarthy
with love

Author's note

The idea for PRUDENCE first came to me in 1967. I wrote it as a long short story called HOUSE OF CARDS and it appeared in serial form in *19*. I took the story and completely rewrote it, and the result is PRUDENCE.

CHAPTER ONE

FOR the twentieth time I said goodnight to Pendle and let myself into the flat. Big Ben was striking eleven. Jane, my flatmate, stretched out in front of the fire, raised a scarlet face to me through a mass of drying blonde hair.

'Any progress?' she asked hopefully, then answered for herself. 'No, obviously not – you look as unpounced upon as ever.'

I went over to the mirror. My curls were unruffled, my lipstick unsmudged. Boasting apart, I looked great. Why then, after twenty dates, hadn't Pendle made a pass at me?

We'd met at a party a couple of months back – a ghastly What-do-you-do-for-a-living?, Oh-I-bash-a-typewriter sort of party, with overhead lighting and someone dishing fruit salad from a huge bowl into our glasses. Pendle and I were the only sheep among a huge crowd of goats, but then they always say the fairest flowers grow on the foulest dung-heaps.

He was not the sort of man you noticed immediately – light brown hair, a thin, expressionless face and pale grey eyes, but he had a detachment and exaggerated cool that was, in itself, a provocation. He wore a charcoal grey suit, of the most irreproachable orthodoxy, grey shirt and a pale tie, but he was tall and very thin, so his clothes looked good on him.

I was wearing my joke kit that evening. I'm very sensitive to clothes. When I wear frills I become demure; in studded leather, I stride around and act butch, but when I wear my joke kit – orange Bermudas with braces and a cheesecloth shirt. I scintillate and tell jokes. When Pendle came over and joined our group, I rattled off three jokes in quick succession

9

that had everyone except him falling about, so I moved off to talk to someone else.

The party was given in one of those long, high eau de nihilistic Sloane Square rooms where you always think something exciting is happening at the other end, and it never is. One of the flatmates, Marcia, had even asked her mother. Not that I've anything against mothers in the right context, but at parties they do waste valuable hunting time. And this one was a twenty-stone do-gooder, who'd set like a great pink blancmange on the sofa. Every so often unfortunate guests were clobbered to talk to her.

'Eats, anyone?' said another flatmate, waving a plate under our noses. 'I'm sure *you're* not on a diet, Pru, you're *so* skinny.'

'I'm starving,' I said, spearing a sausage. 'I only had time to grab a sandwich-board man at lunchtime.'

'I do hope I don't pong,' confided the flatmate. 'Marcia filled the bath with ice so none of us could have a bath.'

Next minute Marcia rolled up with two new arrivals.

'I want you to meet Eileen,' she said, introducing me to a large blonde with dirty finger nails, 'who makes absolutely sooper jewellery. I know you'd like some, Pru. And this is Clifford, our firm's accountant, who's very clever with figures.'

'Only some figures,' said Clifford, leering at my too tight Bermudas, then braying with laughter and spraying cashew nuts all over me, between the gap in his front teeth.

I asked Eileen about the 'sooper' jewellery.

'Oh please don't interrogate me,' she said. 'I'm so tired,' and proceeded to describe the entire plot of a film she'd seen that afternoon.

'I work in Harrods,' said a pale girl, 'but in the book department,' as though that made it better.

Then they all talked about President Carter, Mrs. Thatcher, Laura Ashley, and the latest biography by Antonia Fraser, which everyone seemed to have read except me. I know one should try to look vivacious at parties when one's stuck with boring people. Attractive men are always supposed to think what fun you look and come over and introduce themselves; but the man in the charcoal grey suit was showing no signs of approaching me, and any minute I'd be buried alive in cashew nuts. The flatmate came round with the sausages. I drew her aside.

'Who's the man in the grey suit?'

Her face brightened. 'Oh, isn't he lovely? He's called Pendle, Pendle Mulholland.'

'I bet he made that up.'

'He's quite capable of it,' she said. 'Marcia invited him. She says he's absolutely brilliant. Evidently he was called to the Bar younger than anyone else in years.'

'He ought to be called to the bar more often,' I said crossly. 'He hasn't touched his drink. It might make him more jolly.'

I'm a trier at parties, so I chatted up all the draggy men and danced around to the record player, but I was conscious all the time of this Pendle man watching me like a cat.

Perhaps the fruit salad was more potent than I'd thought, because I finally went up to him and said, 'Why don't you have another drink and look a bit more jolly?'

'There isn't any whisky,' he said, 'and the local wine's a bit too vigorous for me, although it's done wonders for that plant.' He pointed to a mauve chrysanthemum in a pot on the table. 'It was quite dead when I arrived.'

I giggled and took another sip at my drink.

'I can't place the tangy flavour,' I said.

'Vim probably. Marcia mixed it in the wash basin. You must have the constitution of an ox,' he added as I drained the glass.

'I'm after the cherry,' I said. 'I hear you're a solicitor.'

'Barrister.'

'I never know the difference.'

'I talk more in court.'

'What did you do today?'

'Defended a wife-basher.'

'Goodness, how exciting. Did you get him off?'

'Naturally.'

'How?'

'By proving his wife was utterly impossible.'

'Was she?'

'Shouldn't think so. That isn't the point,' he said. 'My job was to get him off.'

'Defending the wicked for the sake of worldly gain,' I said. I examined his cold, fleshless, face with its beautiful bone-structure, and strange, grey, unblinking, deep-set eyes. He must look stunning in a wig – Robespierre, the charcoal grey incorruptible.

'I bet you're absolutely lethal in court,' I said.

He gave a thin smile, and told me about a drugs case in which he'd been prosecuting the week before. I found it riveting. I was also fascinated how detached he was.

Then a diversion was caused by one of Marcia's young men who had mistakenly thought it was fancy dress and had turned up as a goat in a furry coat and pink udders. I had had enough to drink by then to think it terribly funny and started crying with laughter. Looking up suddenly, I saw Pendle absolutely devouring me with his eyes.

'Are you taking me for A levels?' I said, groping for a tissue. 'Didn't your mother ever teach you it was rude to stare?'

'I'm sorry. You're extraordinarily like someone I used to know.'

'My boss doesn't like solicitors,' I said. 'He says but for them he'd have had a perfectly amicable divorce.'

'They all say that. What do you do?'

'I'm a copywriter. I sit in an office all day thinking what to put. Then when I finally put it down Rodney, my boss, comes along, changes it all, and pretends it was his idea in the first place. He's been away all week shooting.'

'Grouse?' asked Pendle.

'No. Butter commercials in Devon.'

I'd obviously been hogging the most attractive man in the room for too long because Marcia came up and asked Pendle if he was all right. Bloody rude, I thought. Then she asked me if I was going to the Old Girls' reunion in Pavilion Road.

I said I wasn't. Had I seen anything of old Piggy Hesketh.
I said I hadn't. Then I admired her dress, because I couldn't
think of anything else to say.

'Laura Ashley, of course,' she said smugly.

Red-faced flatmates were now staggering in under piles of
plates towards a table at the other end of the room.

'There's eats whenever you need them,' she said.

Suddenly there was a lot of shrieking and some rugger
types arrived.

'Oh God,' said Pendle.

'I do hope everyone's going to dance again once they've
eaten,' said Marcia. 'I must go and turn up the vol.'

'Dust to dust, Laura Ashley to Laura Ashley,' I intoned,
helping myself liberally to a bottle of Cointreau that had
been left on the table.

I looked at Pendle again, suddenly deciding I wanted him
very much.

'Who was the person you think I'm exactly like?' I said.

He was about to tell me when Marcia came roaring over
saying she must break us up – like a French loaf – because
she terribly wanted Pendle to meet Charles who was a
partner in D'Eath and March. Almost at once the lecherous
accountant, who'd given up spraying cashews and taken
up toast crumbs and pâté, came over and asked me to dance,
so I jigged around with him and had another belt of
Cointreau to keep up my spirits. Then I had some gin and
orange that had been brought by one of the rugger players
for his girlfriend. Then one of the rugger players asked me
to dance and thrust me around like a cocktail shaker.

'If you don't stop, I'll turn into a White Lady,' I panted.

Normally I don't drink much, but Pendle's presence had
jolted me. I knew I was reaching the dangerous stage when
suddenly a wicked alter ego emerges making me cast
smouldering glances at happily married men, and cannon off
groups of people like a shiny red billiard ball. A stockbroker
in a flowered scarf kept turning off the lights. I expected to
see Pendle's eyes gleaming in the dark like a cat.

People were eating now. Despite the fact that the pâté

13

tasted like old socks and the kipper mousse contained more bones than Highgate Cemetery, everyone was sychophantically asking Marcia for the recipe.

'Lots of brandy and garlic,' she was saying.

'Nice tits,' said the rugger player, looking at my nipples. The pockets of my cheesecloth shirt, which usually covers them, had ridden up after all that shaking.

'It's much easier of course if you get your butcher to mince the pork and the pig's liver first, like my butcher does,' said Marcia.

'I'd like a balloon,' I said to one in particular.

'Come back to my little black hole of Belgravia,' said the accountant.

'Then you chop up some fresh thyme,' said Marcia. Suddenly she noticed that her mother was sitting unattended on the sofa, stuffing herself with kedgeree and, grabbing my arm like a vice, said, 'Oh Pru, I know you'd like to meet Mummy.'

Why should I meet Mummy? I was far too busy keeping handsome men in stitches with my witty repartee. I stuck my legs in like our dog when he doesn't want to be bathed, but Marcia was too strong for me – much stronger than any of the rugger players. Next minute I was rammed down on the only tiny corner of the sofa that wasn't occupied by Mummy.

'Lovely kedgeree, Marcia,' said her mother enthusiastically. 'I don't know how you do everything.'

'Oh it's just organization; *you* know that better than anyone,' said Marcia, skipping away like a young lamb and leaving me to my fate. I couldn't see Pendle anywhere.

'You must be very proud of Marcia,' I said insincerely.

'Everyone says that,' said her mother smugly. 'She gets on with everyone, runs the flat, holds down a job, and of course she's Sir Basil's right hand, and then there's all her voluntary work.'

After Marcia she moved on to shopping, rabbiting on and on about triumphant forays to Dickins and Jones, dignified rebukes to shop assistants, the matching saucers tracked down, the jersey with the pulled thread returned. Really I wasn't up to it at all.

Behind her the accountant was making more code signs trying to get me on to the dance floor, and out of the corner of my eye I could see the rugger player waiting to tackle from the left. The flatmate who hadn't been able to have a bath was dancing with the goat, which seemed appropriate. Perhaps they were having a pong-pong match. A couple were necking unashamedly on the next door armchair, the man's hand well advanced into the girl's blouse. I was terrified Marcia's mother would see them. Marcia had turned up the volume to drown the more excessive of the rugger songs and the distant sounds of some of the fruit salad being regurgitated in the lavatory.

I couldn't hear a word Marcia's mother was saying. My only hope was to watch her teeth and laugh when she did. I was in despair; my glass was empty; I thought of sending out maroons. I knew as a copy writer and as a potential novelist I ought to be studying the old monster. One day I might want to put her in the book. The true writer's supposed never to be bored by anyone, but what was the point of studying her if I'd be far too drunk to remember anything about her in the morning?

Suddenly I saw Pendle through a gap. He was talking to the blonde with dirty fingernails, but he was glancing at his watch and had the abstracted look of a referee about to blow his whistle. That decided me.

'I must get you some of Marcia's delicious pudding,' I yelled in her ear, and floundered towards the food table. Marcia passed me going in the other direction.

'Poor Mummy,' she screamed, 'I was just coming to rescue you.'

I ate some kedgeree out of the dish. It was quite good. I licked the spoon thoughtfully and took some more. One of the rugger players tugged off the goat's udders and, to much shrieking, threw them out of the window. Pendle suddenly looked round and caught my eye. He left the blonde and came over.

15

' "I stood among them, but not of them",' I intoned, ' "In a shroud of thoughts which were not their thoughts".'

'You got trapped,' he said.

'I've been taken on a tour of three million department stores. I feel utterly shop-wrecked.'

He didn't smile. I licked the spoon, then helped myself to more kedgeree and ate it. Then I realized how disgusting it must look. I blushed and put the spoon down. The mauve candles bought to match the Michaelemas daisies, which Mummy had presumably brought up from the country, were almost burnt down.

'The rain in Spain falls mainly on the plaintiff,' I said, picking at the battlements of wax. Still not a flicker. Really he was making me feel very edgy with all this staring.

'Pretty fireproof, aren't you,' I snapped. 'Why don't you go if you're so bored?'

He looked at me consideringly for a minute then said,

'I will if you come with me.'

I was so surprised I nearly dropped the saucepan.

'Wild horse-guards wouldn't keep me away,' I said.

Two seconds later, I was burrowing like a dog through all those tweed and camelhair coats to find my bag, panicking that he might change his mind.

Outside the beginning of autumn lay sodden and misty, with a faint smell of dying bonfires in the Chelsea gardens. Conker husks and the kapok innards of the udder lay strewn over the pavement.

He had an expensive looking car, pale grey, of course. I remember there was a half-eaten bar of chocolate in the glove compartment. I ought to have seen the red light then. People who don't gobble up a bar of chocolate in one go have too much self-control.

'Why are you called Pendle?' I said, snuggling down in the front seat.

'After a mountain, not far from our house.'

'I bet it's hell to climb and covered with snow all the year round,' I said, admiring his perfect Greek nose. I'd got hiccups quite badly. 'Not a very good party.'

'I don't like cold houses and warm drink,' said Pendle, 'but it had its compensation. Where do you live?'

'On my nerves and on the edge of Battersea Park. My flat-mate works in publishing. She's lovely.'

'All girls say their flatmates are lovely.'

'She really is. She's having an affair with a married man, going home to bed in the lunch hour and all that.'

'What about you?' he said.

'I play the field,' I said.

It was true. I had plenty of boyfriends at that time, but no one I really cared about. I was poised for the big dive.

The sky was a brooding dappled dun colour; the moon was drifting through the clouds like a distraught hostess. A slight breeze jostled the leaves along pavements and gutters. We were driving along the Embankment now, the river rippling in the moonlight. Such was my euphoria, I didn't realize we hadn't crossed Chelsea Bridge towards Battersea until we drew up at a large block of flats.

'*Ou sommes-nous maintenant?*' I said.

'*Mon apartement,*' said Pendle.

'*Oh la la.* Where's that?'

'Westminster. Very convenient for my chamber in the Temple.'

'Torture chambers,' I muttered. 'I suppose that's where you dream up devilish plots to confound your poor victims.'

Pendle lent across and opened the door for me.

'I don't usually go to men's flats the first night I meet them,' I said.

'I'm sure you don't,' he said calmly. 'I hope you don't usually go to parties like Marcia's.'

'Oh well,' I said, as he locked the car, 'just a quick drink and then home.'

'What floor?' I said, collapsing into the lift.

'Thirteen. Are you superstitious?'

'No, just super.' As I haphazardly pressed a button, Pendle took me in his arms. That first kiss felt so faint-makingly right that it was only when he stopped for breath that I realized the lift had stopped too. Aware that I wouldn't be

17

looking my best with smeared lipstick under overhead light, I scrabbled at the lift gates, then felt very silly when I realized we were still on the ground floor.

Pendle laughed. 'You pressed the wrong button.'

When we finally reached his flat I headed straight for the bathroom for a re-spray. My face was very mussed and flushed. If only I looked as nice after parties as I do at the beginning. To my dismay I then realized I'd left my muck bucket at Marcia's and brought someone else's bag instead. Inside I found a notecase with three fivers, a driving licence, several credit cards, and a photograph of a labrador and a tweedy woman with her legs apart. There was even a diary with the pencil still in the back – and we were now in September. Obviously a well-ordered person. Alas the only make-up she had was an awful cherry lipstick, which was hardly sufficient for the repair job I needed. I peered into Pendle's medicine cupboard hoping for some make-up left by a former or current mistress, but only found expensive aftershave, talcum powder and, what was more interesting, two half-full bottles of tranquillizers and sleeping pills. Perhaps he was much more strung up than he seemed, behind the cool façade.

'Oh well,' I thought, taking the shine off with a bit of talcum powder, and slapping his aftershave on to my pulse spots, 'I'll just have to rely on personality.'

He was standing in the hall. For a minute he stood there staring at me, as though he was memorizing every feature.

'It's incredible.'

'Will I do?' I said, swinging on the door handle.

'A thousand ships,' he said.

'What?'

'Well perhaps 950 ships. A purist would grumble about the freckles, and say your eyes were too far apart.'

I looked bemused.

'Sorry,' he said. 'I've been trained to be infuriatingly enigmatic. It's a game I used to play with my brother Jack. You know, Helen was the face that launched a thousand ships; we used to grade women from 1,000 ships downwards.'

'What's Marcia?' I said.

'She only rates a rather dirty tug boat and a couple of sampans.'

I giggled.

'She won't be pleased. I've walked off with someone else's bag.'

'I seems sad that someone of your tender age should join the criminal classes so early,' said Pendle.

'Will you defend me?'

'M'Lord, the defendant was not in full possession of her senses when the crime occurred.'

'You can say that again. Had I better take it back?'

'Christ no, not tonight. Ring up and say you've got it. The telephone's over there.'

Just as I was dialling, Pendle picked up my hair and kissed me on the back of my neck, sending shivers down my spine.

'Nice hair,' he said. 'Is it natural?'

'Of course,' I said. 'I'm far too young to dye.'

I actually made him laugh. Oh, the wages of scintillation! Then I had to dial the number again.

Marcia was cross. 'We've been looking for it everywhere, and Mummy and I wanted to do the washing up. Where are you?'

'Back home. I'll bring it over first thing in the morning.'

I wandered into the drawing-room which was beautiful, harmonizing greys and rusts, with several abstract paintings with signatures even I'd heard of, thousands of books, and the sort of vastly elaborate hi-fi system you need a licence to drive. He opened a cupboard full of drink. That ought to have been another warning. If Jane and I have a bottle in our flat, we drink it. If there's more than one we give a party.

'What d'you want to drink?' he said.

'A gimlet please,' I said, thinking that would fox him. But he reached straight for the Vodka.

'I'm sorry I haven't any fresh limes,' he said. 'Will lime juice do? I'll get some ice. Put a record on.'

They were all classical, but I by-passed the Bach and the

Bruckner and put on Ravel's Bolero. That beat drives me insane.

He came back and handed me a large drink.

'How delicious,' I said, taking a huge gulp that nearly took my throat off. He poured himself some whisky and sat down on the sofa opposite me. He lit a cigarette and stared at me through the smoke – it was very unnerving. He's the only man I've met who is completely unembarrassed by silences.

'I was at school with Marcia,' I said. Silly that the old bag seemed to be our main point of communication. 'She was always winning prizes for history.'

'She still seems to be buried in the Dark Ages,' said Pendle. 'How do you know her?'

'Her father's a high court judge.'

Oh, so he was ambitious. I started to sing that snatch of Gilbert and Sullivan about falling in love with an old attorney's elderly ugly daughter.

'Not that Marcia's so elderly or ugly really,' I added, quickly remembering that men aren't supposed to like bitchy girls.

'I couldn't do that,' I rattled on. 'Marry someone awful just to advance my career. I don't think I could ever sleep my way to the top.'

The rate I was going downhill, I reflected, I could easily sleep my way to the bottom. I did fancy him, but I mustn't, not on the first night. I was far too tight anyway, and my Bermuda shorts were even tighter; they left the most unattractive creases on my body.

He was still staring at me. I tried to cross my legs, but found they were already crossed. That Bolero was really getting going now. Tum-tutty tum, tutty, tutty, tutty tum, tutty, tum. I was itching to dance – but instead I got up and went over to look at his books. There was some philosophy, some poetry, but mostly law books.

I turned round and, smiling, danced slowly towards him. The music made me feel as though I had long gipsy skirts on. I must have looked an idiot in those Bermudas. I stood swaying in front of him. He watched me through narrowed eyes for a moment, then caught me by the hips and pulled me on to his knees.

Oh dear, I did adore kissing him – but suddenly everything got out of control. He was biting at my lips. His hands were everywhere, ripping off my clothes. He turned completely savage, and I was fighting to get away from him. Then, just as suddenly, he stopped and buried his face in my neck.

'I'm sorry,' he whispered. 'I'm sorry.' It was weird, as though he were talking to someone else. After a few seconds, he got up and took me home and he never made another pass at me.

CHAPTER TWO

In fact I was shattered when Pendle rang me the next day and asked me out, and from then on took me out two or three times a week. As a boyfriend, you couldn't fault him. He always took me to nice places, he rang when he said he would, and was never more than five minutes late. But, somehow, he never opened up with me, and beyond the fact that he dressed well, had a beautiful flat and was already making a name for himself at the Bar, I knew nothing about him.

What I noticed most was his rigid self-control – or was it lack of appetite? He never ate much, pushing his plate aside after a few bites and lighting a cigarette; he never drank much, and always after an excellent dinner and a bottle of wine, when I was expansive, and ready for laughter and love, he would tip the waiter, exactly 10 per cent, gather up his change and take me home.

I tried everything to win him. I leant forward in low-cut dresses, and backward in high-neck sweaters. I put my hair in bunches, in case he was on the Lolita kick. I put my hair up, in case he liked sophisticates. I even faked flu, and wore a see-through nightie when he came to see me. Not a pass was made, not a lecherous grab.

And yet I found this icy reserve ridiculously seductive. Every time I made him laugh I felt I'd conquered Everest. I had also seen him moved to tears by a Beethoven Quintet. The whole time I was aware of the banked fires beneath the icy reserve, of a tension just this side of menace. As the weeks passed I found myself getting more and more hooked on him.

Jane and I discussed it interminably.

'Perhaps he's a pouf,' said Jane.

'That was no pouf who attacked me the first night.'

'Perhaps he's married and doesn't want to compromise you.'

'That's never deterred any married man I know.'

'Perhaps he's shy.'

'Shy? He's the coolest thing this side of an iceberg.'

'So – perhaps he's serious and doesn't want to muck it up after the first night's fiasco.'

'Wouldn't that be lovely?' I sighed. 'I'll ask him to dinner and you can tell me what you think.'

Dinner was a catastrophe. Usually I love cooking, but the evening Pendle came round I tried too hard. I asked Rodney, my boss, who's a bit finger-snapping and aggressively trendy, but a giggle when he gets tanked up, and another smashing zany girl copywriter from the agency called Dahlia, who can be guaranteed to make any party go. Jane had asked a man she fancied in her office, who was very witty as well as being a Liberal M.P. All week I had fantasies of Jane and I sitting round looking radiant by candlelight, and contributing the odd remark as the conversational ball bounced scintillatingly along.

Usually when people came to dinner, we ate lounging on cushions in front of the fire, and Jane made jokes about having to lay the floor, but that night I polished up the gate-leg table, and laid it with candles and flowers. When Jane arrived home. I was rolling out pastry with a milk bottle.

'How's it going?'

'All right, except I've made too much.'

'Never mind. Henry can't come, so I've asked this fantastic guy I met at a party last night. He's called Tiger Millfield. Isn't that great? And he plays rugger for England, so I'm sure he'll eat for at least fifteen.'

'Oh dear, I hope he and Pendle get on.'

'What's in here?' said Jane, tripping over a casserole on the floor. There was so little room in our kitchen.

'The filet for the boeuf en croute, mopping up a vat of Nuits St. Georges,' I said airily. 'Now everyone can say I marinaded beneath me.'

Jane groaned. 'You have got him bad. Candles, flowers, gin, whisky. Jolly good thing it's the beginning of the month. What else are we having?'

'Pâté and tomato salad to start with, then the beef, and peaches soaked in white wine to finish up with.'

Jane's mouth watered. 'What about the finger bowls and the waterlily napkins?' she said. 'I'm surprised you aren't dressing Rodney up as a butler.'

I ignored her and went into the drawing-room to give the gate-leg table a last polish with my skirt.

'Do you think I ought to put Pendle or Rodney on my right?' I shouted. 'Rodney's been married. Does that take precedence over a bachelor?'

'I really don't know. I'd better go and change into something suitably gracious.'

'There's still masses to do,' I wailed.

'Well I'd better not distract you then.'

Somehow at five to eight I was ready. I'd even bought a new dress for the occasion, long and mediaeval looking, in rust-coloured velvet, with an embroidered panel at the front, and long trumpet sleeves. I kept having another fantasy about Pendle staying long after everyone else, drawing me into his arms and saying, 'Really, there's no end to your achievements.'

'That's nice,' said Jane, admiring the dress. 'The Lady of Shallot! Appropriate too, after all those onions you've been chopping. You'd better take the price off.'

Jane was wearing very tight jeans, no bra, and a blue T-shirt, which matched her blue eyes, and made her nipples stand out like acorns. She looked far better than me. My beastly face kept flushing up and clashing with the rust.

Bang on the dot of eight, the doorbell rang. Jane picked up the answer-phone.

'It's Pendle,' she said, 'raring to get at you.'

With shaking hands, I put a new Purcell record on the gramophone.

Jane giggled. 'Are we all going to dance the Gavotte?'

Initially I could see Jane was impressed by Pendle. He was wearing a grey pinstriped suit which fitted his long greyhound figure to perfection, and his cold seagull's eyes looked at her without any of the enthusiasm she was accustomed to from men. Here was a challenge. I made a lot of fuss pouring his whisky, running back and forth for water and ice. Usually Jane and I talked ninety to the dozen, but his presence seemed immediately to shut us up.

'Do you think you'll win the Westbury case?' I said, after a long pause. I had been following it in *The Times*.

'We might,' said Pendle, 'if Lady Westbury can be persuaded to go into the box.'

'Sounds like a horse,' said Jane.

'Why?' said Pendle.

'Well some horses are difficult to get into horse boxes, or loose boxes,' she added, brightening. 'Do you ride?'

'Yes,' said Pendle.

'Well you must know it's called a box. Oh, forget it. Pru says you've got a gorgeous flat in Westminster.'

'Yes.'

'That must be fun. Lots of M.P.s smuggling in their mistresses. Did you ever meet John Stonehouse?'

'No,' said Pendle.

'Don't they invite you to orgies?'

Pendle in fact didn't respond at all and made no attempt to chat her up. The pauses in the conversation became longer and longer. It was with passionate relief that we heard the doodle bug tick tick of a taxi arriving, and an explosion of voices and car doors slamming in the street below. It must be Rodney.

'He's bringing Dahlia,' I said. 'She's lovely.'

Rodney arrived with two litres of Pedrotti and no Dahlia. She had evidently got flu. Instead he had brought a beautiful but unbelievably dreary girl from the Publicity Department called Ariadne who lived on weed salads and yoghurt and was permanently talking about diets.

Rodney, a confirmed lecher, had suffered a great shock when his wife had suddenly left him, and had consequently,

25

by way of compensation, taken up even more dedicated lechery and the wearing of self-consciously trendy clothes. Tonight he was resplendent in a dark green velvet cat suit tucked into black boots, and slashed to the waist to show a blond suntanned chest. (He had just been filming in Ibiza.) The suit was a little too tight for him. I wished he'd worn something slightly less outrageous. Pendle was looking at him with distaste, Jane in wonder.

I was in such a state I forgot Ariadne's name when I tried to introduce her. She needed livening up with a good strong drink, but she insisted on just having water. Had I any idea how many calories there were in alcohol?

'Oh come on, live a little,' said Rodney.

'I've lost three inches off my hips since I gave up booze.'

'Oh Bottom thou art translated,' said Rodney.

Jane shrieked with laughter. Rodney sensed an ally.

'What's this crap you've put on the record player?' he said turning to me.

'Purcell,' I said, blushing.

'Well it won't wash,' he said, winking at Jane. 'For God's sake take it off and put on something less rarefied. Who else is coming?' he said, counting the places.

'Tiger Millfield,' said Jane.

'The international?' said Rodney. 'I was at school with him. We sat next to each other in chapel for three years.'

'What was he like?' said Jane.

'Never spoke to each other.'

Jane and I laughed. Pendle's face didn't flicker.

Rodney took a belt at his whisky and made a face.

'You've put tonic in, darling, instead of soda. You must be in a state.

'You've had a terrible effect on her,' he added, grinning at Pendle. 'She's supposed to flip through the Nationals every morning to see if any of our clients get a mention. All she does is pore over the law reports. Says they're even better than *Crossroads*.'

'Oh, shut up Rodney,' I said.

'We've worked together for two years,' Rodney went on,

'so if you want any gen on her, I'll give it to you – at a price. Perhaps in return you could give me some advice about my divorce.'

'I don't do much divorce work,' said Pendle, coldly. 'I'd consult a solicitor if I were you.'

The rudeness was quite blatant. Pendle obviously thought Rodney too silly for words. He got up and looked at the books – far too many of them cheap novels.

Rodney shrugged and winked at Jane, who winked back.

'Pru never said you were this pretty,' he said, sitting down beside her and admiring her tits. 'Have you ever done any modelling? I think you'd have a great future.'

'I haven't had a bad past,' said Jane.

'I swear by a glass of hot lemon juice first thing in the morning,' said Ariadne.

'I swear automatically first thing in the morning,' said Rodney. 'I don't need lemon juice.'

I escaped to the kitchen. Suddenly there seemed a hell of a lot to do. Making the Bearnaise sauce, unwrapping the butter, uncorking bottles of wine, putting on the potatoes and the *mange-touts*. Two strong drinks didn't seem to have done anything but make me clumsy. I felt myself getting redder and redder in the face. Oh, why had I been so ambitious? The beef would be ruined if Tiger Millfield didn't arrive soon.

When I got back Jane and Rodney were nose to nose admiring each other's cleavages. Pendle was looking grey with boredom. Ariadne was saying, 'I tried the meat and citrus fruit diet, but it made my breath smell.'

I couldn't face them. I escaped into the kitchen again, and was just shaking a lettuce out of the window when Jane joined me.

'Don't leave them,' I wailed.

'Isn't he fantastic?' said Jane.

'Pendle?' I said brightening.

'No, Rodney.'

'What do you think of Pendle?'

'He doesn't exactly make one feel at home, does he?'

27

'Do you think he fancies me?'

'Hard to tell. He never takes his eyes off you, but it's like a cat watching a mouse.'

'Don't you think he's devastating?'

'Not my type really. Let me have about me men that are fat. Yon Pendle has a lean and hungry look. He thinks too much. Such men are dangerous,' she finished off, pleased with herself at the comparison.

'Why haven't you shelled the peas?'

'They're *mange-touts*,' I snapped. 'Well he may not be your type, but what about me?'

'I preferred your other boyfriend – Charlie, even old Tom.'

'Charlie and old Tom were slobs,' I said, shaking the lettuce so furiously that I let go of the cloth and it went sailing out into the street. 'Now look what you've done.'

'Never mind, there's so much to eat,' said Jane soothingly.

'Where the hell's Tiger got to?' I snapped.

The doorbell rang.

Rodney picked up the answer-phone in the drawing-room. 'It's the grandest Tiger in the Jungle,' he said.

'I must go to the loo,' said Jane, disappearing into the bathroom. I knew perfectly well she'd gone to tart up.

As I went to answer the door, there was a terrible crash. Tiger had tripped over all the twenty-five milk bottles I'd put outside in my giant tidy-up for Pendle. He swayed in the doorway with a lettuce leaf on his head. He was very handsome, but also quietly and extremely drunk. Cross-eyed, he confronted his diary.

'Think I've been asked to dinner.'

'Hello darling,' said Jane, coming up and kissing him. Removing the lettuce leaf from his head, she took him into the drawing-room and introduced him.

'Was it a good party?' said Rodney, looking at him speculatively, sizing up the competition.

'Think so,' said Tiger. 'My cigarette packet's absolutely covered in telephone numbers.'

'It's always been my ambition to play rugger for England,' said Jane.

'Mine is to go to work every day reading a pink paper in the back of a chauffeur-driven Rolls-Royce,' said Rodney.

'Mine is to weigh seven stone,' said Ariadne.

Rodney, bent on sabotage, poured Tiger the most enormous whisky. Pendle was looking at his watch.

'We'll eat in two seconds,' I said and hared back to the kitchen for a last-minute panic of dishing-up. My mediaeval sleeves trailed in the Bearnaise sauce, which had started to curdle. Oh, why hadn't I stuck to jeans? I was frenziedly mashing the potatoes when Rodney came in.

'I love the way your bottom wiggles when you do that.' I gritted my teeth.

'Cook is obviously getting a little unnerved,' he went on.

'The same intelligence is required to marshal an army as to cook dinner.'

'Well, I'm not officer material,' I snapped.

'I do like your flatmate,' said Rodney. He peered into the Bearnaise sauce. 'I didn't know we were having scrambled eggs.'

'Too many cooks spoil the brothel,' said Jane. 'I think we ought to eat, Pru darling. Pendle and Tiger are getting on like a piece of damp blotting paper on fire.'

'Go and sit people down,' I said, 'and make sure Pendle doesn't get the side plate with the rabbits running round, or the three-pronged fork.'

'Mind out,' said Jane, pulling Rodney out of the way, 'or you'll be run over by a passing capon.'

'Who's going to say grace?' said Jane, as we sat down.

'Give us this day the will to resist our daily bread,' said Rodney. 'I've put on a stone in the last three months. I used to be lithe as a panther.'

'Let me have about me men that are fat,' said Jane, meaningfully.

'Have some pâté,' I said to Ariadne.

'No, I won't thank you very much. It looks delicious though.'

Now we were in the awful hassle of 'Have you got butter, toast, pâté, tomato salad, pepper? Watch out, the top's inclined to fall off. Oh dear, you haven't got a fork; you must have left it in the tomatoes.'

The table was much too small, and everyone was jabbing elbows into everyone else. Ariadne, having nibbled one piece of tomato from which she had shaken all the oil, was watching every bit of food that went into everyone's mouth like a slavering dog.

'People don't realize how fattening cheese is,' she said to Pendle. 'No thank you, I won't have any wine.'

Tiger and Rodney having established they were at school together were swapping anecdotes across me. Jane was hanging on their every word, and not taking any notice of Pendle who was sitting opposite me. I daren't ask him about work, as I knew Jane and Rodney would start mobbing me up. Suddenly our eyes met, and he gave me that swift wicked smile, and for the first time that evening I felt like not cutting my throat. Stick with me baby, I pleaded with my eyes, I'm not enjoying it any more than you are. But the next moment he had turned back to Ariadne, who was talking about some diet book that had just been published. 'Butter's evidently quite all right in moderation,' she said. She was awfully pretty; perhaps he fancied her.

Tiger's elbow kept falling off the table, and we all had to wait while he ploughed through a second helping.

'D'you mind if we look at the box during the News at Ten break?' asked Rodney, who had several crumbs in his hairy chest. 'I want to see the Virago Tyre commercial. I keep missing it. Have you seen it?' he added to Pendle.

'I don't watch television,' said Pendle.

Rodney flipped his lid. 'That's what I've got against lawyers,' he howled. 'Your attitude is positively antedeluvian. How can anyone not watch television in this day and age?'

Oh God, he was about to launch into his anti-legal profession tirade. I leapt to my feet.

'Could you pass your plate up, darling?'

But Rodney was not to be halted, and when I staggered in

with the beef en croute five minutes later he was still at it.

'My own divorce would have been perfectly amicable; my wife and I might even be struggling on together today if it hadn't been for lawyers putting their oar in. Everyone should conduct their own defence.'

'Oh rubbish,' I said. 'If Eve had had a decent counsel, we'd probably all still be living in paradise.'

I thought that was quite a bright remark, but no one took any notice. They didn't like Pendle. They were waiting for Rodney to carve him up.

'Lawyers are a lot of incompetent hacks,' said Rodney, 'blinding people with their own mumbo jumbo. All you care about is reputation. You don't give a bugger about the issues of the case; you just want to beat other lawyers.'

'That's right,' said Jane.

'I think P.L.J.'s a rip-off,' said Ariadne hopefully. 'No pastry thank you, Pru.'

Pendle sat very still, looking at Rodney, the expression on his face too complex for me to read its meaning. In spite of twelve hours marinading, the boeuf en croute had over-cooked to the consistency of horse meat. Only Tiger seemed to have no trouble with it.

'The people who control our courts,' went on Rodney, splashing wine into everyone's glasses, 'are a lot of geriatrics in fancy dress. The whole system, in fact, is designed to isolate them from the pressures of modern life. Who, pray, are the Rolling Stones? Christ you're cushioned against reality.'

'We deal with murders, rape, divorce every day,' said Pendle mildly. 'I'd hardly call that . . .'

'Exactly my point,' interrupted Rodney. 'You can only deal with the horror of life by turning it into a play with a stage and a cast in period costume.'

'We haven't got any napkins,' said Jane, leaping to her feet.

Rodney was warming up now. 'Why do legal costs increase as the price of a house increases, although exactly the same amount of paper work is involved? Why can't you go

to four different lawyers and get estimates for their services?
And it's all geared to the rich, isn't it? Pay a fine or go
to prison, so the rich pay up, and the poor have to go
to jug.'

'Napkins anyone?' said Jane, coming in with a roll of loo
paper and proceeding to break bits off for everyone. I put my
head in my hands.

'It's time for drastic reform,' said Rodney, tipping back his
chair. 'The crime rate's going up and up, the divorce rate's
rocketing and parasites like you are cleaning up.'

Pendle was playing with his knife. Pale, ascetic, watchful,
beside Rodney and Tiger he looked like a Jesuit priest among
a lot of debauched jolly Cardinals.

'The reason why crime is going up,' said Pendle softly,
'is because people have never before been so well informed
about what they're missing. And we've got your profession to
thank for that. Everytime we turn on a television set, or walk
down a street, or go in the tube, we're bombarded by
advertisements, tempting us with the promise of a better life.
As a result everyone thinks they've got a right to a modern
kitchen, a new car, a beautiful girl in a cornfield, a happy
family life, children in permanently white jeans, a bouncing
bright-eyed dog. No wonder marriages break up when people
are constantly bombarded by an idealized picture of marital
bliss.'

'Oh don't give me that old crap,' spluttered Rodney.
'Advertising provides a service; we tell the public what's on
the market.'

'Rubbish,' said Pendle. 'You create discontent, envy and
avarice. You encourage a constant desire for novelty. Change
the packaging, sell the product as new.'

'Everything is backed up by market research and statistics,' said Rodney pompously.

'Advertising people use statistics like a drunk uses a lam-
post,' snapped Pendle. 'For support rather than illumination.
What sort of world d'you think you've created when there's
no child whose unhappiness can't be dispelled by a sunshine
breakfast, no romantic set-back that can't be cured by using

a new kind of toothpaste, no marital dust-up that can't be ended with a box of chocolates?'

He was playing with words now.

'Bravo,' I said.

'Advertising's fun; no one takes it seriously,' protested Jane.

'Oh yes they do,' said Pendle. 'Thousands of people write in for an amazing offer of a £2 so-called steak knife that's worth 99p. Dress anyone up in a white coat and the public think he's an unimpeachable authority. I came across an advertisement the other day which claimed its product was used by 90 per cent of actors who play doctors on television.'

'Sounds like the sort of line I write,' I said in a desperate attempt to lighten the atmosphere.

'At least advertising keeps people in work – actors, writers, designers,' stuttered Rodney.

'Advertising stultifies creativity,' said Pendle crushingly. 'That's why hardly any decent poetry or painting or music's being produced in this country at the moment. All the creative talent is being frittered away in advertising.'

There was a silence. Tiger Millfield let out a huge belch, but no one giggled. Somehow when Rodney had attacked Pendle it had just been bluster, but with Pendle one felt it was the real thing. It was too late to do any rescue work. I really ought to catch the eye of the highest lady of rank, and whisk her out of the room, leaving the combatants to their port, but we hadn't had pudding yet.

'I'm sure some of the advertising for slimming products is very suspect,' said Ariadne.

'Isn't it time for your commercial, Rodney?' said Jane.

'Well if that concludes the case for the prosecution,' said Rodney, getting to his feet and switching on the box, 'I think we might indulge in a little animated corruption.'

I cleared away. It was sad that people could leave more on their plates than you appeared to have given them in the first place. I didn't bother with the pudding, and by the time I got back with the coffee, the commercial break was over, and Jane and Rodney were stuck into some political scandal on the news. Tiger Millfield was listening owlishly to Ariadne yapping on about wheat germ. Pendle was looking at his watch.

'Where's your glass?' I said.

'I must go.'

'But it's early. Now beastly dinner's over we can relax.'

'I've got to drive down to Winchester early tomorrow morning. The brief only arrived this evening. I haven't studied it yet.'

He nodded a curt goodbye to everyone else, and I followed him out into the hall.

'Will you be down in Winchester long?' I said, suddenly overwhelmed by desolation.

'A couple of days. Thank you for having me.'

'You certainly floored Rodney,' I said. 'I didn't know you felt so strongly about advertising.'

His eyes gleamed wickedly.

'I don't. If I'd wanted to I could have argued the case for advertising just as well.'

'B-but you were so convincing,' I said.

'That's my job.'

And he was gone, without even saying he'd ring me.

Back in the drawing-room Tiger Millfield was trying to ring for a taxi on the answer-phone. In the end he decided to go and flag one down in the street, taking Ariadne with him, thank goodness.

'You get so tired on a diet,' she said. 'Are you coming, Rodney?'

'I'll stay on a bit,' said Rodney. 'Mustn't break up the party all at once.'

I left Rodney and Jane, and went into the kitchen. I felt near to tears, physically and mentally exhausted. The hostess with the leastest, Mrs. Utterly Beaten. A pile of pots, pans, glasses, plates and uneaten food greeted me. I couldn't face it. I went back into the drawing-room. Rodney was sitting in an armchair, rolling a joint, telling Jane about the pot he grew in his back garden. Jane was leaning against his knees. They stopped talking when they saw me.

'Lovely dins, darling,' said Rodney.

'I'm sorry about the beef,' I said, flopping into an arm-chair.

'You were had by the butcher,' said Jane.

'I never know if meat's tender just by looking at it,' I said. 'It all looks the same, like Chinamen.'

'Rodney's going to put me on a poster,' said Jane. 'You're going to see me hoarding down from every stare.'

There was a long pause. Then they both said simultaneously,

'Darling, he's not for you.'

'Why not?' I said, blushing.

'Because he's a bastard,' said Rodney.

'It's only because he worsted you in an argument,' I said. 'He didn't really mean what he said about advertising, he admitted it outside in the hall. He could've just as easily argued *for* advertising.'

'That's what's wrong with him,' said Jane, 'he's inhuman.'

'Beneath that cold chilly legal exterior,' said Rodney, 'is an even chillier legal heart.' He handed Jane the joint; she inhaled deeply.

'I don't know why he didn't go and sit in the fridge,' she said with a giggle. 'Might have warmed him up a bit.'

She offered it to me, but I shook my head. I felt too miserable.

'Come on, cheer up,' said Rodney. 'There are plenty more cold fish in the sea.'

'But I don't want to go out with a fish. Why does he keep asking me out?' I said with a sob.

'I don't know,' said Rodney. 'He's obviously far more interested in his own briefs than getting into yours.'

'If he really cared for you,' said Jane, 'he'd have made an effort to be polite instead of freezing us out.'

'Whatever he feels for you,' said Rodney, much more gently, 'it isn't the normal healthy lust a man feels for a beautiful normal girl. He's playing games with you, Pru, and I don't reckon he's up to any good.'

CHAPTER THREE

WHATEVER game Pendle was playing, he left me to stew after the dinner party. He didn't ring me for a fortnight. I kidded myself he must be working hard, probably out of London. I tried to forget him, but instead spent a lot of time sobbing in the bath and composing long quotation-loaded letters of renunciation in my head. An added irritation was that Jane was having a riproaring time, going out every night mostly with Rodney.

On the Monday evening, a fortnight later, she was getting ready for yet another date, trying to repair the ravages of a weekend of dissipation in front of the drawing-room mirror, while I sat slumped on the sofa, eating my way through a box of chocolates.

'You'll get spots,' said Jane, squirting blue liquid into bloodshot eyes.

'Do you know what I'm sitting on?' I stormed.

'W-what?'

'The shelf. I am hurtling towards spinsterhood and middle age without even a whisker of a supertax husband on the horizon. D'you know how long it is since I've been out with a man?'

'What about Mark?'

'He's not a man, he's a stockbroker.'

I got up and wandered into the kitchen next door.

'I doubt if anyone will ever ask me out again. I must face up to a future looking after cats in an attic. I've definitely decided to give Pendle up.'

'Good,' said Jane.

'At least I would, if he'd have the decency to ring me up, so I could tell him so. I've got nothing to do. And no one to do nothing with. I think I shall buy a dog.'

I opened the fridge, and found a jar of pickled onions. I ate five.

'If he asked you out, I bet you'd go,' said Jane, trying to paint out the purple circles under her eyes.

'I would *not*. Not if they stripped me naked and wild horses dragged me four times round the world, through the forests and across the burning deserts.'

I ate another pickled onion noisily. The telephone rang. I must have qualified for the Olympics, hurtling across the room. It was Pendle. He apologized – but not quite enough – for not ringing before, he'd been impossibly busy. Had I eaten? Would I like some dinner?

An hour later, my curls still wet from a hasty washing, I sat in Julie's bar, lapping up a large glass of wine, and talking out of the corner of my mouth like a gangster, so as not to asphyxiate Pendle with the smell of onion. He looked even rougher than Jane, his face greyish-green with tiredness, his eyes heavy-lidded and red-rimmed. I hoped it was from poring over legal documents not loose-living. When I first saw him I wondered why I'd been eating my heart out for him. Then, as the wine curled down inside me, the old magic started working again.

'Have you had any exciting cases?' I asked.

'Just routine stuff, but I've got a big case coming up tomorrow.' He smiled slightly. 'Defending a rapist.'

After the way he'd tried to pull me the night we'd met I was tempted to point out that he must have plenty of experience in that field. But it seemed a shame to rot up the evening so early on.

'Will you get him off?'

'The odds are against it. My client's a man called Bobby Canfield. He's sales manager of a small export-import firm in the city. He's charged with raping,' he lowered his voice slightly, 'Fiona Graham.'

I whistled. 'Rick Wetherby's girlfriend? But she's ravishing.'

'Ravished you mean,' said Pendle.

Rick Wetherby was a very successful racing driver,

absolutely dripping with charisma and money. His affair with Fiona Graham had been well publicized in the papers.

'Weren't they about to get married?' I said.

Pendle nodded. 'Bobby Canfield was her boss. She claims he asked her to work late – the day before she was due to give up work actually. Rick Wetherby turned up unexpectedly to collect her from work, and found the door locked. She claims Canfield had raped her.'

'How exciting! Had he?'

'Well, they definitely had it off. I've got to prove it wasn't rape. The Wetherby clan are naturally out to hammer Canfield, and they've got the money to do it. They've hired Jimmy Batten to prosecute. He's one of the best Q.C.s in the country. Canfield should have got a Q.C. to represent him too. I'm not really a big enough shot, but I handled his sister's divorce a year back and I suppose he was impressed by that. He says Fiona Graham was absolutely asking for it. But it's going to be a bugger to prove.'

'Girls don't usually "Ask for it" when they're about to marry something as luscious as Ricky Wetherby,' I said.

'Exactly,' said Pendle, 'And Canfield's got a shocking reputation with women.'

He held up his hardly touched glass of wine in the shaft of light from the table lamp, rocking it in the thick glass so it looked almost black. His eyes were just dark hollows now in a white drawn face.

'It's your big break,' I said, wonderingly. 'Aren't you terrified?'

He grinned and filled up my glass. 'Absolutely shit-scared.'

'It'll be packed out,' I said wistfully. 'I wish I could come and hear you.'

'You can if you like,' Pendle said. 'If you can get the day off I'll save you a place in court.'

If the onions hadn't been making a come-back, I'd have kissed him then and there.

There was a heavy frost that night. Next morning, smothered in Jane's red fox fur coat, I walked to the tube.

Each twig and blade of grass glittered with whiteness. The last yellow leaves covered the parked cars and crunched like frosted cornflakes beneath my feet. Outside the court the crowds shivered and stamped their feet. They were mostly motor racing fans, anxious to catch a glimpse of Ricky Wetherby and his beautiful fiancée. For the sake of procedure her name was supposed to be kept a secret, but everyone knew who she was.

Once inside I was utterly turned on by the theatrical atmosphere of the packed courtroom, the rows of journalists lounging and exchanging gossips, the solemn beefy policemen and the array of wigs and robes. The Judge, in scarlet, was a little mole-like man with bright eyes and a twitching inquisitive nose. He looked capable of ferreting out the truth, and not likely to stand any nonsense.

Opposite, sitting in the vast dock, was Bobby Canfield, raffish, handsome, his face slightly weak about the mouth and chin, his hair thinning and too long at the back. And there was Pendle, even paler than ever, but outwardly calm and looking sensational in a grey wig and gown.

James Batten, Q.C., a sleek, dark, dapper otter of a man in his early forties, opened for the Prosecution, and for half an hour in magnificently sculptured prose had the privilege of so blackening Canfield's character that before a word of evidence was heard there seemed no longer any doubt about his guilt.

'In the dock, ladies and gentlemen of the Jury,' he said in tones of fastidious horror, 'is a man charged with a revolting offence, a typing pool Don Juan who took advantage of this inn-o-cent girl, so in love with her handsome fiancé that there was no other thought in her head but her marriage in a few weeks' time.'

Canfield's face was expressionless, but there was a muscle going like a sledgehammer in his cheek, and he was twisting his signet ring round and round his little finger. You could see Batten had impressed the Jury. Oh poor Pendle, I thought in anguish, what chance has he got?

'I shall now call my first witness, Miss Graham,' said

Batten, smoothing his sleek hair with an air of anticipation. The Press and public gallery licked their lips. Fiona Graham did not disappoint them. She came into court wearing a grey wool dress with a white collar, a Hermes scarf attached to her Gucci bag, her shoulder-length blonde hair brushed back from a smooth forehead. With her blue eyes downcast, and a slight flush on her beautiful pink and white complexion, she indeed looked the picture of inn-o-cence. I thought the white puritan collar was overdoing it a bit, but there was no doubt the Jury were impressed. As she took the oath in a whisper, you could feel the waves of approval and sympathy. Even the Judge looked more benevolent.

Batten rose with a reassuring smile.

'Do you recognize the man in the dock, Miss Graham.'

She bit her lip, looked at Canfield, gave a shudder and said she did. Then in a clear, but occasionally quavering voice, aided by much sympathetic prompting from Batten, she told the court how Canfield had asked her to stay late, as he was going to be out of the office next day, how he waited till the building was deserted, then tried to kiss her. Running to the door she had found it locked, whereupon Canfield had ripped her dress open, forced her back on the desk and proceeded to rape her. Afterwards when she was still sobbing hysterically, there was a hammering on the door. After telling her to straighten her clothes, Canfield had opened the door and found her fiancé and Miss Cartland, the head of the typing pool, outside.

'My fiancé then insisted I went to the police,' she whispered. 'I didn't want to.'

With a sob in her voice she went on to say how excited she had been about the wedding. She was so beautiful and so touching, you could see the pity on everyone's face; two of the women jurors were surreptitiously wiping their eyes.

In this emotionally charged atmosphere, Pendle rose to cross-examine.

'Hasn't a dog's chance,' muttered a fat woman on my right, offering me a glacier mint.

Pendle, too, reassured Fiona Graham with a slight smile. His voice was quiet and gentle in direct contrast to Batten's histrionics.

'When this unfortunate event occurred, you were getting married in six weeks' time?'

She nodded.

'I think we could all agree your fiancé is a rich man?'

'Yes, he is.'

'In fact, marriage to him would represent a considerable change in your circumstances?'

It was almost indecent the caress Pendle could get into his voice. Listening to the soft unhurried syllables, Fiona began to relax, her pretty white hands with their colourless nails unclenched on the Gucci handbag.

'I gather you've been working for Mr. Canfield for three months, that you came as a temporary and stayed on? Was that because you liked Mr. Canfield?'

'No. Not especially, but he wasn't in the office much, and I liked the other people who worked there.'

'As you were marrying such a rich man, with so much to do before the wedding, was it strictly necessary to go on working?'

Fiona Graham's eyes widened.

'I wanted to be independent. My fiancé's given me so much. I'm not married to him yet. My mother's a widow and she hasn't got much to pay for the wedding. I wanted to help out as much as I could.'

The Jury nodded sympathetically. Pendle examined his finger nails.

'If you needed money,' he said softly, 'why didn't you get a job nearer your flat, where the fares would have cost you less, and you could have earned more money? After all temporaries can get up to £80 a week, but I gather you were only getting £45 working for Mr. Canfield.'

'When one's getting married,' said Fiona sweetly, 'there's so much to think about. It's a strain adjusting to a new job. I'm not a very good typist. I thought it would be less hassle to stay where I was.'

41

'Better the devil you know,' said Pendle. 'Did you find Mr. Canfield attractive?'

Fiona Graham shuddered.

'No,' she said sharply. 'Anyway I'm not interested in other men. I love my fiancé.'

'In fact you disliked Mr. Canfield?'

'I didn't dislike him, I was embarrassed the way he looked at me.'

'In what way?'

'Well,' she blushed, 'as though he wanted me.'

'Then why did you work late?'

'I wanted to do my job properly,' she said with a sob. 'I never dreamed he'd abuse my trust.'

She was like Little Nell, little death knell where Pendle was concerned. The Jury were looking at him with loathing. He seemed unmoved.

'You claim that the evening the so-called assault occurred, Mr. Canfield ripped your dress open and a button came off. What happened to the button?'

'I don't know,' she whispered. 'I w-wasn't in a fit state to . . .'

There was an agonizing pause; then Pendle said in a voice of ice.

'Earlier you told my learned friend you were crying hysterically because the defendant had taken advantage of you, and this crying was overheard by Miss Cartland who runs the typing pool, and later by your fiancé?'

'That is correct.'

'I suggest,' hissed Pendle, 'you were crying because you were caught in a trap. The wedding was only six weeks away, your financial set-up necessitated making a rich marriage, but you suddenly discovered you weren't in love with your fiancé at all, but infatuated with Mr. Canfield.'

Jimmy Batten leapt to his feet.

'M'Lord, I *must* protest.'

Fiona Graham burst into tears. 'It's not true,' she sobbed. 'I love Ricky. I hate and detest Mr. Canfield.'

There was so much desolation in her voice I thought Pendle was going to get lynched.

'Cold-blooded bastard,' said my fat neighbour. 'I bet he treats women badly.'

'He does,' I said, accepting another glacier mint.

Pendle picked up a piece of paper.

'Does the name Gerry Seaton mean anything to you?'

Suddenly Fiona was still, like a wary animal, but her tone was flat when she answered, 'I don't know what you mean.'

'It's a simple question,' said Pendle politely. 'Do you or do you not know a man called Gerald Seaton?'

'I have never heard of him.'

'You didn't spend a weekend with him in the Cotswolds on July 30th and 31st this year?'

'Certainly not.' She allowed herself a little hauter now.

Batten was on his feet again. 'My Lord,' he said wearily, 'I hardly see this is relevant.'

'Get back to the point, Mr. Mulholland,' said the Judge.

'No more questions,' said Pendle and sat down.

Fiona Graham was followed by an impressive array of prosecution witnesses, including the office crone, shivering with venom, all hammering another nail into Canfield's coffin. Pendle battled valiantly with each one, but didn't make much headway.

Finally, to the excitement of many of the crowd who recognized him, Ricky Wetherby went into the box, and was so handsome, godlike and suntanned, and so distressed in a stiff upper-lipped way that within seconds the whole court was on his side.

'And that concludes the case for the prosecution,' said Batten. Ricky Wetherby stepped down. The judge looked at his watch, and we adjourned for lunch.

Pendle stopped for a few words with Canfield and his poor shattered wife, and then joined me outside.

'You were great,' I said. 'I never dreamed you'd be that good.'

43

He shook his head. 'It's going to be rough this afternoon. Come on, we've only got an hour.'

It was still bitterly cold, but a weak sun shining through thin clouds like a sullen pearl had melted most of the frost. A few typists were feeding the pigeons as the taxi bowled through Lincoln's Inn Field. Our destination was a hot steamy little pub with dark-panelled walls, which seemed to be full of lawyers. I was about to say how nice it was when I stiffened, for there at the bar, downing a large whisky stood Jimmy Batten.

'Look,' I hissed.

'I know,' said Pendle.

Jimmy Batten turned round and smiled at us.

'You made it. What can I get you?'

'A large whisky please,' said Pendle. 'You can afford it too, out of the vast fee you're no doubt getting out of the Wetherbys. You had a bloody good morning.'

'Might go either way,' said Jimmy Batten with unconvincing modesty.

'I must say you do dump your clients with indecent haste,' said Pendle. 'You ought to be reported to the Bar Council. You can't have spent more than ten seconds reassuring the lovely Miss Graham. I thought you might bring her in here for a drink.'

'Oh she's far too inn-o-cent for dives like this,' said Jimmy, winking at me. 'Aren't you going to introduce me to this ravishing creature?'

I was gazing at them both open-mouthed.

'But you've been sneering and glaring and hissing at each other all morning,' I gasped.

'I know,' said Jimmy. 'It's part of the act, shows we're trying. What can I get you to drink?'

'A large gin and tonic, and her name's Prudence,' said Pendle, giving me a cigarette. 'You were in rare form, Jimmy; all those references to Tarquin and Lucrece.'

'Have to give the Jury their pornographic kicks,' said Batten, 'only way of keeping them awake.'

44

'I suppose you're going to butcher my client this afternoon?'

'I'm going to carve him up, my dear. Ice and lemon?' he added, handing me my drink, 'And doesn't he deserve it?'

'Pru thinks he's innocent,' said Pendle. 'She's with me, and don't forget it.'

I'd never known him so friendly. Perhaps it was because Batten was so important.

'She's much too pretty to waste herself on a cold fish like you,' said Jimmy, his merry dark eyes sparkling, and stroking my fur coat as though I were a cat. I found him very attractive; he had all the assurance of the older man, but none of the pomposity.

'Since you find her so alluring,' said Pendle, 'would you mind feeding and caring for her while I nip back to chambers and sign some documents?'

'Delighted,' said Jimmy Batten with such alacrity that it took away some of my disappointment at Pendle sloping off. After all, all the women's magazines encouraged one to get on with *his* friends.

'Don't listen to a word Jimmy says,' said Pendle, running a finger down my cheek. 'Lawyers are the most frightful gossips.'

And he was gone. I felt myself go crimson both at the unexpected caress, and the speculative way Jimmy was looking at us.

Jimmy and I ate shepherd's pie and shared a bottle of wine, crammed thigh to thigh in a panelled alcove. Jimmy was blissfully easy to talk to – particularly as he was just as interested in yapping about Pendle as I was.

'I never expected him to be that good,' I said.

'He's brilliant. Mind you, he's a bit too cool to go down well with a jury. He hasn't got an easy ingratiating personality, and he knows it, but he's good at asking questions. He doesn't say anything really offensive, but before the witness knows what's happening he finds himself tied up in knots.'

'He did it with my boss the other night. It brought the entire dinner party to a halt.'

Jimmy grinned. I noticed how many laughter lines he had on his face. It was sad Pendle had none. 'I admire the way he never gives up on a case,' he said, filling up my glass. 'I bet he's up to something now, trying to rootle out a piece of evidence that'll blow my case sky-high. Not that it'll do him any good; it's obvious as hell Canfield's guilty. Has he been taking you out for long?'

I knew he was pumping me now. I must be careful.

'Since the summer.'

'It's the first time I've seen him with a girl.'

'That's nice,' I said.

'I sometimes wondered if he weren't a bit the other way,' said Batten, idly, 'and he's working hard to sublimate it.'

'Queer you mean?'

He shot me a sidelong glance and nodded. 'He refers to "the lovely Miss Graham", for example, but he's totally unmoved by her.'

'Oh no,' I insisted in horror. 'He's certainly not queer.'

'You've got proof, have you? I must confess if you belonged to me, I couldn't keep my hands off you. Have an enormous brandy and tell me more. I'm sorry to keep staring at you, not that it's not a pleasure, but you remind me of someone and I can't for the life of me think who it is.'

'Pendle said that the first night we met,' I said.

I had an uneasy feeling he knew a lot more than he was letting on, and such was the warmth of the room, and the amount I'd drunk and the cosiness in his manner, I was tempted to pour out my anxieties about Pendle. Then I remembered about lawyers being terrible gossips. I wasn't sure I trusted Mr. Batten, so I changed the subject.

After lunch it was the turn of the defence. As Pendle rose to his feet, straightening his gown and the papers in front of him, his hands shook, but he spoke calmly enough.

'We intend to prove that my client has been the victim of a monstrous calumny. Not only has he been charged with a revolting offence, he has also lost his job, will no doubt have difficulty finding another one, been publicly humiliated, and privately diminished in the eyes of his family and friends – and all this on the testament of one girl. Her word against his. Her fiancé arrived too late and found a locked door. What we have to find out, ladies and gentlemen, was what went on beyond that door. Intercourse,' he paused. 'We have no doubt; the police medical report bears this out, but at whose instigation. Miss Graham looks like the innocent flower, but is she perhaps the serpent underneath?' He paused again for effect and glared at Jimmy Batten who glared back, his lip curling with disdain.

I was hard put not to giggle.

Even as he took the oath, Canfield gave the impression of being a con man, a rep with his shiny shoe in the door. The Jury were looking at him with disgust.

Pendle stared at him thoughtfully.

'Mr. Canfield, was Miss Graham a good secretary?'

'No,' said Canfield.

'Why did you keep her on then?'

Canfield smiled wryly. 'I suppose I was attracted to her.'

There was a ripple of chattering round the court.

'I told you so,' muttered my fat neighbour, handing me a pack of Maltesers.

'You wanted to sleep with her?' said Pendle.

'In a word, yes.'

'But refrained from doing so?'

'She was engaged to be married. I do have some principles. Besides, Ricky Wetherby is much bigger than me.'

It was a bad joke which did nothing to endear Canfield to the Jury.

'And what happened on the day of the so-called assault?'

'She said she'd lost her notebook; could I possibly dictate the letters I'd given her yesterday again. I said I had to go to a meeting. I came back at 5.30 and told her to come into my office.'

'What was Miss Graham wearing?'

'She'd changed into a new dress; it was very becoming.'

'Can you describe it?'

'Well it was very low cut, and made more so because she'd lost a button.'

'What happened then?'

'I said she looked smashing; was she going to meet her fiancé? She smiled and said not until much later. I said he was a lucky man, and we'd better get on with the letters or we'd both be in trouble. Suddenly she burst into tears, said she felt trapped, that her fiancé was a disaster in bed.'

There was a murmur of protest from the public gallery. The Judge told them to shut up. Fiona's face was expressionless.

'We heard a step outside. Fi – I mean Miss Graham said please lock the door, and then she went on crying. I told her she was crazy to marry him feeling like that. I put my arm round her to comfort her.'

'Did she offer any resistance?'

'God no, quite the reverse. She said she'd wanted me for weeks. The next minute we were on the floor.'

'And intercourse occurred?'

'It certainly did.'

The rustling and coughing always present in court had died away. People were leaning forward not to miss a word.

'Thank you, Mr. Canfield,' said Pendle, and sat down. He seemed surprisingly elated, particularly since Batten took over next, and absolutely tore Canfield to pieces. Although Canfield stuck to his story, it looked pretty ragged by the end. White and shaken, he sat down.

Next Pendle called one of the pretty typists from the office. She came in giggling and patting her hair, and wearing far too much make-up. Pendle handled her with the utmost gentleness and soon her nerves disappeared.

'We were both in the Ladies getting ready to go home. It was about 5.15. Fi – I mean Miss Graham was changing into this lovely dress, very low cut. She said she was going to meet her fiancé later. At that moment a button popped off, which made it almost, well, indecent.'

'You're sure of this?'

'Course I'm sure. She said that was the trouble with buying cheap clothes. I offered to lend her a needle. I said once she was married to Ricky she wouldn't have to buy cheap clothes any more. Besides, it looked more sexy without the button, and we had a giggle about that.'

The tension was beginning to mount in the court. The Jury were sitting up and taking notice.

The next witness was blond, handsome and brash, and said his name was Gerald Seaton. He described himself as a commercial traveller.

'Have you seen Miss Graham before?' said Pendle.

'Yes, we met in the King's Cross Hotel lounge exactly four months ago.'

'How did you meet?'

'She picked me up.'

Suddenly the court went very still.

'I was working on some figures. She came and sat near me, and smiled at me. I smiled back. She was a very pretty girl; she said she was meeting her aunt off the Leeds train, but it had been delayed. We arranged to meet next evening.'

'Did she tell you she was engaged?'

'Oh yes, she made no secret of the fact. She was going to marry this rich bloke. Said he was no good in bed.'

I glanced at Ricky Wetherby. He looked as though he'd been turned to stone.

'What happened next?'

'I took her away to the Cotswolds for the weekend. We stayed in a hotel.'

'How did you pass the time?'

'We spent it in bed.'

'Even though she was engaged to be married?'

'Didn't worry her; why should it worry me?'

Jimmy Batten, looking rather grim, got up to protest.

'Surely, My Lord, this is utterly irrelevant. These events happened long before my client met the defendant.'

'I can assure you it has the utmost relevance on the case,' said Pendle quickly.

'Proceed Mr. Mulholland,' said the Judge.

'What happened after this weekend?'

'We met once; then she suddenly refused to see me, pretending she'd decided not to cheat on her fiancé any more. Well that didn't wash with me after her performance in the Cotswolds. So I waited for her outside her office one evening.'

'Her new office?' said Pendle.

'Yes. She must have been working there about a fortnight. We went and had a drink; she got a bit bombed, and then it all came out. She'd got a thing about this bloke at work, said she was mad about him, but he refused to do anything about her.'

'Do you remember what his name was?'

'I can. It was the same village near my home. He was called Canfield, Bobby Canfield.'

There was not much Batten could do with Mr. Seaton, nor did he have much joy with the hotel manageress in the Cotswolds, who remembered Fiona and Gerry Seaton staying there.

'They signed in as Mr. and Mrs. Seaton. I remembered her because she was so pretty. We didn't think they were married. I mean they stayed in their room all weekend. We just took their meals up.'

The Wetherby Camp looked thunderstruck. Next moment Fiona was on her feet.

'They're lying, they're all lying. It's a frame-up.'

Jimmy Batten put out a hand to hush her and, rising to retrieve the situation, said smoothly,

'M'Lord, I should like my client to go back into the witness box to refute these charges.'

The Jury looked shaken and undecided.

Fiona went back into the box. She had regained her sang-froid now. She denied that she had ever been away for the weekend, or even met Mr. Seaton. There must be some mistake. She remembered she'd had a bad cold that weekend, her fiancé had been abroad, so she'd stayed in bed without going out for two days.

'It's a conspiracy,' she said, her eyes filling with tears again. 'I swear I've never set eyes on this man in my life.'

The barometer was wavering once again. I felt the Jury were going to believe her.

There was a long pause. Then it was Pendle's turn.

'Miss Graham,' he said in his gentlest drawl, 'you do realize that people who don't tell the truth in court can be sent to prison?'

'Of course,' she said.

Pendle crossed the court and handed her a piece of paper. 'Did you write this letter?'

She glanced at it. 'Yes, it's a thankyou letter for a wedding present.'

Pendle went back to his place.

'My Lord, I have here a document in the same writing as this letter. Later I will call a handwriting expert to verify their similarity. Normally I wouldn't resort to snooping and appropriating private documents, but when my client's reputation is at stake . . .'

'All right, Mr. Mulholland,' said the Judge irritably, 'get on with it. What have you got to show us?'

Pendle picked up a kingfisher-blue, leather-bound book, which had been hidden in his papers; the lock was hanging from it.

'I have here a diary belonging to Miss Graham in which she chronicles only too clearly the events of the past few months.'

Suddenly Fiona's face twisted in horror. 'No, don't let him,' she screamed. 'He's got my diary; he's a thief.'

'Be quiet, Miss Graham,' snapped the Judge. 'Proceed, Mr. Mulholland.'

Jimmy Batten's face never moved an inch, but he must have felt the floor give way beneath him.

'M'Lord,' he protested, 'I must object to my learned friend's methods.'

'I'm sure you do,' said the Judge. 'Go on, Mr. Mulholland.'

'In a minute the ladies and gentlemen of the Jury can examine the diary themselves,' said Pendle, 'but first I'd like to read out one or two passages.'

The lack of expression in his voice made Fiona's passionate

outpouring sound even more dreadful. First there was her description of meeting Gerald Seaton and the weekend in the Cotswolds exactly as he had described them.

' "It's marvellous",' he read in his flat drawl, ' "after Ricky, to find someone who knows what he's doing in bed." '

Fiona's lips were blue now. 'It's a forgery,' she whispered.

Pendle flipped over a few pages : 'Now,' he said softly, 'let us turn to her description of her first days of working for Mr. Canfield : ' "My new boss is really sexy, I fancy him rotten." Here on the 5th is a picture of Mr. Canfield cut out of the *Investor's Chronicle.*'

'Nothing unusual in that,' snapped Jimmy Batten. 'Any girl would cut out a photograph of her boss.'

As detail followed horrendous detail of her growing obsession for Canfield, I couldn't bear to look at her, or at Ricky Wetherby, sitting stunned and unbelieving. I was mesmerized by the distaste and cruelty in Pendle's voice. How he seemed to hate her. I could only think of a cobra striking again and again.

'And now,' he said suavely, 'if you'll bear with me, I'll read the entry on September 28th, the day before the alleged rape :

' "Bobby's wife came in today. God I loathe her, the old frump. Bet she bores him to death in bed. Tomorrow is my last chance. I shall die if I don't get him. If only Ricky'd let me go on working after we're married. I'll wear my new blue dress, and pretend I've lost my shorthand notebook and ask Bobby to give me the letters again after work. If we're alone in the building, something's bound to happen. I know he fancies me." '

Against my will, my eyes went to Ricky Wetherby, and came away again at once. It was crucifixion.

Pendle paused again, and looked slowly round the court. 'After this the diary becomes rather anatomical, and moves into the realms of fantasy as to what Miss Graham would like Mr. Canfield to do to her in bed. I imagine the ladies and gentlemen of the Jury would find it less embarrassing to read for themselves.'

But the next moment Fiona had jumped down from the

witness box and was crossing the well of the court towards Pendle, screaming abuse.

'Bastard! Bastard! Give it back to me!'

I thought she was going to claw Pendle's face, but Ricky was too quick for her. He was beside her in a flash, his handsome face stone-grey as a pavement.

'Leave her alone,' he shouted at Pendle, putting his arms round Fiona. 'Say it's not true, Fiona darling, for Christ's sake, say you didn't write it.'

For a minute she glared at him.

'Yes, I did,' she hissed. 'I wrote every word of it. Can't you understand that I love him? I love him!' And she collapsed, sobbing hysterically, into the arms of a policewoman.

A great sigh went through the court. For a minute the Jury conferred. Pendle was about to call his next witness. But the Foreman of the Jury forestalled him. If it so pleased His Lordship, they felt they had the evidence required.

'What witness were you about to call, Mr. Mulholland?'

'A handwriting expert, M'Lord.'

The Foreman consulted with the Jury again.

'M'Lord we have reached our verdict already. We are unanimous in returning a verdict of Not Guilty.'

'Always thought she was a fast piece,' said my neighbour, disconsolately, upending the empty red Malteser packet.

The Judge in his summing up congratulated Pendle on his handling of the case, admiring his tenacity, if not his slightly reprehensible methods of obtaining information. The moment he swept out in his scarlet robe pandemonium broke out. Fiona Graham was led away by the police and the Press made a most indecent dive for the public telephones outside. Across the court Pendle was being congratulated by a stunned Canfield contingent. His hands were shaking as he gathered up the papers. I knew he was dying for a cigarette. Looking up, he caught my eye over the crowd and waved. I made a double thumbs up sign. Then he mouthed that he was a bit tied up, but he'd pick me up at the flat at 8.30.

I took a bus to Sloane Square, and then walked home. I wanted some fresh air and time to think. Women in tweed skirts were raking up leaves in Chelsea gardens. An aeroplane trail was turning pink in the setting sun. Inside the houses, people were switching on lamps and lighting fires. A group of children were throwing sticks into a goldfish pond; a black spaniel ran round them barking with excitement. It all seemed so normal after the dramas in court. I was haunted by Ricky Wetherby's stricken face. He had been so God-like and self-confident that morning. I kept thinking of Pendle, cruel and as merciless as Torquemada, turning and turning the thumbscrew on Fiona Graham. In a kinky way, though, the whole day had been so erotic. Fiona's feverish craving for Canfield had been uncomfortably near to my own feelings for Pendle. If he didn't make a pass at me soon, I should burst. I had been rattled too by Jimmy Batten's comments. Perhaps Pendle *was* queer, and if so what was the point of seeing any more of him? But after today, I knew I was in too deep to get out. I felt restless, uneasy and horribly carnal. I'd better have a cold bath before I went out.

In fact we had a heavenly evening; all my fears were lulled. Pendle took me to Parkes and we sat in a secluded corner, guzzling champagne and Mediterranean prawns fried in garlic, and gloating over the evening papers. Canfield had been vindicated at great length, with the most sensational headlines.

'How on earth did you get that diary?' I said, holding out my empty glass absently. Pendle filled it.

'I spent the last fortnight chatting up Fiona's flatmate.'

'Is she pretty?' I said, bristling.

'No.' Pendle flipped my nose teasingly with his finger. 'She's a cow and absolutely eaten up with jealousy where Fiona's concerned. She pretended it wasn't quite cricket to hand over the diary. Actually she was frightened Fiona'd find out she'd nicked it.'

'When did she finally give it to you?'

'Lunchtime today.'

I whistled.

'I did run it a bit close, I admit. That's why I had to abandon you to Jimmy's blandishments. You made a conquest there.'

'Did I? How lovely.'

'He rang up when I got back to the office, ostensibly to congratulate me, actually to ask us both to dinner next Friday.'

'Ooh, can we go?'

Pendle was silent for a minute, fidgeting with his lighter. That was odd; I'd never seen him fidget before. Then he took a deep breath.

'I'm thinking of going home for a few days next week. I was wondering if you'd like to come too.'

For a few seconds I couldn't believe my ears. I was so overwhelmed I couldn't speak.

'I'd adore to,' I finally squeaked.

Relief seemed to flood over him.

'It's a long way. My family live in the Lakes, but it doesn't take that long up the Preston Motorway. I'd like to leave on Thursday afternoon, and probably come back on Sunday night. Can you get the time off?'

'I've still got some holiday left,' I said. 'And I can always blackmail Rodney by threatening to tell Jane terrible things about him.'

'Good. We'll try and make it in time for late dinner then.'

'It'll be such heaven getting out of London,' I said.

He smiled rather ruefully. 'I hope you'll enjoy it. They're all rather formidable, particularly my mother.'

I went whooping into the flat, dying to tell Jane all about it and barged into the drawing-room. In the dim light, I could just distinguish two people locked on the sofa.

'Get out!' shrieked Jane. She must have picked up someone at the party she'd been to. How crude, I thought loftily, as I made myself a cup of coffee. How much more sensible Pendle and I were conducting our affair. I'd obviously destroyed their mood, for a few minutes later I heard voices, and the front door bang. Jane came into the kitchen looking ruffled.

'You look jolly smug,' she said sourly. 'Has he asked you to marry him?'

'Not quite,' I crowed, clutching my happiness to me like a hot water bottle, 'but he's asked me to stay with his family next week.'

For a second her face fell. However much one likes one's flatmate, one can't bear their love-life to go too well, but Jane is basically a nice person, and she smiled almost immediately.

'Pru, that's marvellous! When? For how long? What on earth did he say? Tell me all. He must be serious, to take you home to meet his mother.'

I muttered something about chickens before they're hatched. But I found it difficult in the next few days to keep my mounting elation in check, and wrote Prudence Mulholland all over my shorthand notebook.

CHAPTER FOUR

JANE became very bossy.

'If Pendle says his mother is formidable, she must be a tartar. She's bound to go through your things when you and Pendle are striding over the Fells, to see if you're a slut or not. You'd better buy some new underwear – I counted two safety pins in your bra – and a new nightie, in case Pendle comes stealing down those dark passages after lights out.'

'You must be joking,' I said, but I could not suppress a shiver of excitement.

In the end, she did my packing for me.

'Tissue paper always impresses people,' she said. 'And lots of little polythene bags for your sweaters.' She insisted that I bought a pair of lace-up shoes.

'But I've got a perfectly good pair of boots,' I wailed.

'Kinky,' she added darkly. She lent me a silk dress, but refused to let me take any of my more outrageous clothes.

'You want to borrow them while I'm away,' I grumbled. 'I'll look such a frump, Pendle won't recognize me.' But I managed to sneak in my green culotte dress when she wasn't looking.

'Now remember,' she warned me, 'lots of housework, clean the bath, don't wipe your make-up off on the towel and, for God's sake, don't smoke in bed. These old houses burn down very easily. You'd better take my knitting too.'

'But I can't knit,' I protested.

'That doesn't matter. Just take it out of its bag from time to time and count a few stitches. It gives the right impression.'

'You seem to know a lot about it,' I said nastily. 'Where did it get you?'

'The mothers adored me,' she said airily. 'It was the sons who went off me.'

Pendle picked me up at the office about five. He was wearing a dark grey sweater, which emphasized his pallor.

'If we don't hit heavy traffic' he said, putting my luggage in the boot, 'we should be there by nine.'

He was smoking incessantly and seemed very much on edge. We didn't talk much, then my tummy started rumbling. I hadn't eaten since breakfast.

'There's a slab of chocolate in the back,' he said. I found it and, as Pendle wasn't hungry, wolfed the lot and then felt sick.

'Before we get there,' I said, licking my fingers, 'can we sort your family out a bit?'

'Pretty complicated,' he said, 'but I'll try and explain. My father, as you know, is dead, and I'm the eldest. Then there's my sister Linn, who has emotional problems and works in Manchester, so she probably won't be be there. Then there's my younger brother Jack. He's only twenty-eight but he's already on his second marriage. He used to be a terrible rake, but he's running the family firm now and seems to have settled down. With Jack you have to take the smooth with the smooth, but you'll like him. Everyone does.' There was a trace of bitterness in his voice.

'What's his wife like?' I asked.

'Maggie? Very young, very spoilt. I don't think she's very nice but, like Jack, you can't help liking her. They're staying with my mother until their house is built.'

'So there'll be your mother, Maggie and Jack,' I said, ticking them off on my fingers.

'And, to confuse you further, there might be Ace.'

'Who's he?'

'My step-brother. My father was married before, but his wife died when Ace was a baby.'

'Poor little boy. Who brought him up?'

'My father wasn't the sort to stay a widower long. He

married my mother almost immediately, and we were all brought up together.'

'Is he married too?'

'Ace? He was – but his wife was killed in a car crash two years ago. She was driving to meet him at the airport. The roads were icy.'

'Oh, how awful.' I said.

'Ghastly. Particularly as she was pregnant. He absolutely worshipped her. We all did. We never thought anyone would be good enough for Ace, but she was.'

Pendle had never sounded so enthusiastic about anyone.

'What did he do after that?'

'He was working for *Panorama* in London, then he landed a job in New York for American television. He roves all over the world. He hasn't been home since Elizabeth died, but my mother said he might possibly be back this weekend.'

The conversation dwindled. I slept fitfully, and wondered if it would be worth letting my head slip on to Pendle's shoulder, but thought better of it. As a few stars made a tentative appearance, I speculated about Pendle's brothers – Jack, the reformed rake whom everyone liked; Ace, whom no one was good enough to marry.

A slim white moon slipped between the stars. We were now driving over cobbled streets. When we stopped for petrol, a blast of icy wind came through the door.

'Not far now,' said Pendle. 'We'll be there in twenty minutes.' The hills began to grow into mountains. I've always been frightened by mountains, and I suddenly shivered as I wondered what I really knew about the silent, withdrawn man beside me. I put on some scent to give me confidence. Beside the road, there was a gleam of silver.

'That's Grasmere,' he said. A few minutes later, he swung off the road up a winding drive.

The headlights showed heavy undergrowth, and brambles hanging in festoons on either side.

'Here we are,' he said, hooting his horn.

I could only see that the house was large and hung with

creepers. As we opened the car doors a black labrador and a large English setter came bounding out, wagging their tails and barking amiably. The front door opened and we were flooded in a stream of light. I was quaking with nerves as I saw an old woman standing in the doorway. She had an apron on. Pendle's mother. I walked forward smiling.

'Hello, Mr. Pendle,' she wheezed. Obviously *not* Pendle's mother.

'Hello, Mrs. Braddock,' said Pendle.

'It's good to see you back, after so long. Come into the warm.'

Mrs. Mulholland must be a cold customer, I thought, not to come rushing out to welcome him. I knew what my mother was like whenever I came home. I followed Mrs. Braddock into the hall, which was huge and baronial and covered in faded crimson wallpaper.

'I'll just help Mr. Pendle with the cases,' she said.

A moment later, Pendle followed me. He looked furious – a muscle was twitching in his cheek.

'I'm afraid my family aren't here. They've gone to a party in Ambleside. So we'd better eat now. I'll show you your room. I expect you'd like a wash.'

I'd been so steamed up to meet his mother, it was a terrible anti-climax. I followed him upstairs, along a dark, winding passage to my room.

'I'm sorry. It's frightfully cold in here,' he said, drawing the curtains and turning up the central heating. If only he had taken me in his arms then and there everything might have been all right.

'It's lovely,' I said. 'I'll just clean up and come down.'

On closer inspection, I found it wasn't at all lovely. None of the drawers had been cleaned out : there was only one broken coat-hanger – and even I, who never notice dust, couldn't miss the thick coating on the dressing table. I couldn't imagine my mother having anyone to stay and not giving them flowers. The only compensation was the large double bed. I was strangely chilled by that room. However I re-did my face and calmed my wild curls a bit.

In the dining-room I found places had been laid for Pendle and me at opposite ends of a long table. Mrs. Braddock served us watery soup. It's incredibly difficult to drink soup quietly in a huge empty room, and then we had stale game pie, and cold potatoes which stuck in my throat. Luckily, Pendle opened a bottle of wine.

'Mrs. Braddock's been with us for years. Her husband looks after the garden and the stables. I don't know who else would put up with my mother.'

The two dogs sat on either side of me, drooling at the mouth. Then the setter put a large speckled paw on my knee.

'They're lovely,' I said. 'What are they called?'

'Wordsworth and Coleridge,' said Pendle. 'Coleridge is the setter. I don't expect anyone's remembered to feed them.'

I was relieved when he picked up both his and my game pie, gave one to each dog and then lit the inevitable cigarette. The wine was stealing down me, and I began to perk up.

We had coffee in the drawing-room, which was also huge and shabby and full of beautiful things. A bowl of dahlias which had seen better days were shedding their petals on the smeared table. On one wall there was a large square of much lighter red wallpaper, where a picture must have recently hung.

'Oh God,' said Pendle, 'my mother must have flogged the Romney. Ace will do his nut.'

I huddled by the fire, clutching Coleridge for warmth. A fat orange cat was asleep on the sofa.

'Her name's Antonia Fraser,' said Pendle ruefully. 'Have some brandy.'

'I oughtn't to,' I said. 'I don't want to be tight the first time I meet your mother.'

'Well, I'm going to,' he said, 'so you might as well.' I noticed his hand was shaking as he poured out two glasses. He was so jumpy, he was making me more and more nervous. I was just about to examine the photographs on the desk when I heard voices and doors slamming.

'Here they are,' said Pendle. He'd gone as white as a sheet. We went into the hall. The front door was thrown open. A very beautiful woman stood in the doorway. She was as slim as a blade.

'Darlings,' she cried, rushing towards us. 'How awful you must think us. We didn't think you'd be here for hours.'

Jack's wife? Pendle's sister?

'This is my mother,' said Pendle.

My jaw clanged like a visor.

'But you can't be!' I said. 'You're too young.'

Fatuous remark, but she was delighted.

'This is Pru,' said Pendle.

'You must call me Rose,' she said taking my hand. 'Oh, look. Naughty Coleridge has moulted all over you.'

She probably hadn't altered her style of dressing for twenty years, but she was bang in fashion now, with rippling blonde waves, round eyes and a tiny scarlet mouth. She'd have set them by the ears in the King's Road too, in that marvellous fifties crepe-de-chine dress. I felt absurdly self-conscious in my twinset and tweeds.

She didn't look so young in the drawing-room, but she quickly switched off the overhead light and put on two side lights.

'How are you, Pen, darling? You look tired. Have you been overworking? Such a good party – Maggie and Jack are still there.'

'I thought I heard voices outside,' said Pendle.

Rose looked sheepish. 'James Copeland dropped me off.'

'Linn's James Copeland?'

Rose nodded.

'Oh God,' said Pendle. 'Is he after you, too?'

'Well, a bit. Too embarrassing really. My daughter Linn gets so cross when her young men run after me,' she added to me.

I stared at her, fascinated. I'd never known a mother like this – skipping around in raver kit, pinching her daughter's boyfriends.

'Do get Primrose and me a drink, darling,' she said to Pendle.

'Her name's Prudence,' said Pendle acidly. 'And she's got a drink. When's Ace coming back?'

Rose turned her eyes to the ceiling.

'Oh, don't remind me – the day after tomorrow. No, don't glare at me like that, Pen. You know I'm fond of Ace. But he makes me feel so hopeless and he's bound to nag about money.'

'How is money?'

'Oh, disastrous as ever. Look how shabby everything is.' She picked at a piece of cotton wool oozing out of the yellow sofa. 'Jack and Maggie's house is costing the earth.'

Another car drew up outside, more doors slammed and we heard voices in the hall. Pendle's face was expressionless, but once again that muscle was twitching in his cheek.

'Don't spend all night,' said an irritable male voice. The door was pushed open and a man walked in. His face creased into an incredulous smile.

'You're here! Already! You must have blown a gasket on the motorway.'

Pendle looked rather ostentatiously at his watch.

'It's already eleven o'clock,' he said.

'God, is it that late? I *am* sorry.' He turned to me.

'This is my brother Jack,' said Pendle.

Jack Mulholland was outstandingly good-looking and already going to seed. He had terrific bags under his eyes and was beginning to put on weight under the chin. Tall and broad-shouldered, he had those blue, sexy bloodshot eyes that looked as if he'd been swimming under water too long; and he knew how to use them. He looked into my face for a minute, then very slowly ran his eyes over my body, then back to my face again, as though he had to memorize every detail. A smile spread over his face. 'At least 1,000 ships. But then you always had excellent taste, Pen.'

I squirmed with embarrassment and pleasure.

'Where's Maggie?' said Rose.

'Re-doing her face.'

'Darling, do get us drink,' said Rose.

Jack filled up our glasses, and poured two more for Rose and himself.

Pendle raised his eyebrows. 'Pru's not a great drinker.'

'Don't be a spoilsport,' said Rose. 'Well, here's to you, darlings, and a happy weekend.'

'That was bloody good, you getting Bobby Canfield off,' said Jack. 'Everyone's talking about it round here.'

'Mrs. Braddock's started a scrap-book of your cuttings,' said Rose.

I took a sip of my drink and nearly choked. Through streaming eyes I caught Jack laughing at me. He *is* attractive, I thought. The moment he comes into the room the temperature goes up. At that moment a girl came in, and the temperature shot even higher. She was everything fashion magazines say you shouldn't be. Her brilliant red hair looked as though it had been cut with garden shears. She wore so much eyeliner her eyes slanted into her ears, and she was falling out of a dress two sizes too small for her and jacked-in at the waste with a green leather belt.

But she was gorgeous. Any man confronted with that glowing vitality would want to tear those terrible clothes off her and tumble her into bed.

She stood in the doorway staring at Pendle. All of a sudden the room became very still. The colour drained out of Pendle's face.

'Hello, Maggie.' His voice was curiously dry. 'You look well. This is Pru.'

She turned and smiled at me. Her eyes were like headlights. I wanted to blink.

'How odd,' she said slowly. 'She looks rather like me.'

I blushed. I looked like a ghost beside this buxom radiant creature.

'Not odd at all,' said Jack with a slightly twisted smile. 'Mulhollands always go for redheads.'

Maggie sat on the arm of Pendle's chair.

'Get me a drink, Jack,' she said, and, as Jack went over to the drinks tray, added quite audibly, 'You shouldn't have stayed away so long, Pen.'

Something funny was going on, but I was too tired to work it out. The brandy was sending me to sleep. I hardly listened as they swapped family gossip. I was only conscious that, beneath the superficial banter, there was an underlying tension. It was Jack who noticed I was falling off my chair.

'Poor little Pru's half dead. For goodness' sake take her up to her room, Pen.'

I staggered to my feet. 'Don't bother, I can easily find my own way.'

'Will you be all right?' said Pendle.

'Of course she won't,' said Jack, leaping up and taking my arm. 'Come on, lovie, say goodnight to everyone.'

It was arctic in the hall.

'You go on up,' said Jack. 'I'll try and dig you out a hot-water bottle.'

After a few false starts, I found my room. I hardly had the energy to undress and take off my make-up.

I laughed as I remembered Jane's instructions about folding my clothes up neatly. That lot downstairs wouldn't care if I strewed them all over the landing. By the time Jack came upstairs, I was sitting in bed in my new black nightdress.

'I'm afraid I've drawn a blank on the hot-water bottle,' he said. 'Will you be warm enough?' he added, standing by the bed and looking down at me.

'I'm fine,' I said. I was coming out in goose pimples, but it wasn't because of the cold.

'You look very fit for human consumption,' he said, examining my back. 'You're still brown.'

'It's always the bits that don't show that last longest,' I said slowly.

Jack Mulholland undoubtedly had a way with women, like some people have with animals. He made them relax. Before I realized it, he'd put a warm hand on my bare back and, bending down, kissed me slowly on the mouth.

After a moment he broke off, but his hand was still caressing its way down my back. Goodness, he's lethal, I thought. Get a grip on yourself, Prudence. He's the sort of man who'll stop at nothing.

'Wow,' said Jack dreamily. 'You're gorgeous,' and he was about to kiss me again when a familiar voice said, 'Everything all right?'

I pulled away from Jack as though I'd been stung.

Pendle stood in the doorway. His face was as enigmatic as ever. That's done it, I thought. I wonder how long he's been standing there.

Jack laughed. He didn't seem remotely embarrassed.

'Oh dear, I've lapsed again,' he said. 'I'd better ring up Redheads Anonymous.'

CHAPTER FIVE

I was woken next morning by rain like machine-gun fire
on the roof and Coleridge and Wordsworth lying on my feet.
The curtain let in long fingers of light across the ceiling. I
looked at my watch. It was eleven o'clock.

I had a bath and dressed. No one was about downstairs. I
went into the drawing-room. Last night's jetsam of glasses,
cigarette ends and coffee was still lying about.

I pulled back the musty, dark blue, velvet curtains and
caught my breath at the desolation of the scene before me.
Down below in the valley was a huge, black lake, and all
around like dark, sleeping beasts lay the mountains, their
peaks shrouded in mist.

The garden was a wilderness of tangled shrubbery. Lichen
crawled over the paved terrace – and I'd never seen such
rain, sweeping in great curtains across the lake, stripping the
last leaves from the trees, flattening the blackened dahlias.
There was no colour except where the beech trees still
smouldered among the dark pines.

This is Pendle's country, I thought, country that would
put winter into anyone's soul. Oh God, I did hope he wasn't
upset about Jack kissing me last night.

Remembering Jane's advice about helping in the house, I
gathered up the glasses and cups, found the kitchen and
washed them up – not so easy as there was no washing-up
liquid.

Where on earth was everyone? I was dying for some
coffee. Suddenly I heard a noise and, poking my head out of
the kitchen door, saw a tall man with a black and grey
flecked crew cut wearing a college scarf and a tweed jacket
tiptoeing towards the front door, carrying his shoes. I

couldn't see his face. The next moment he'd opened the door and shot out closing it very quietly behind him. He must be one of Rose's boyfriends. I went back to the drawing-room and had another look at that terrifying view.

'Drinking it all in?' said a voice. It was Maggie, in a dressing-gown. She didn't look so ravishing this morning, deathly pale with her mascara smudged underneath her eyes.

'You haven't got a cigarette, have you?' she asked. 'Jack's gone over to the mill with Pendle and I've run out.' I got a packet out of my bag and handed it to her. She lit a cigarette with a trembling hand.

'God, I needed this. We rather overdid the boozing last night.'

'What a fantastic view this is,' I said.

Maggie shrugged her shoulders. 'It gives me the creeps, particularly on days like this. I want to go back to London, but Jack's so keen on the mill, I suppose we're stuck here for good.'

I asked her if I could make a cup of coffee.

'Oh, hell, it's Mrs. Braddock's day off, so everything goes to pot. Tomorrow she's got to blitz the house from top to toe. Ace is coming home. He'll be appalled at the state of the place.'

She looked round, grimacing at the sticky rings left by glasses all over the furniture, the peeling paint, the dead flowers.

'That's the odd thing about my mother-in-law,' she went on, 'as long as she can have stunning clothes and pay her bridge debts, she doesn't mind if the house falls to bits.'

We went into the kitchen. Antonia Fraser jumped off a chair and started weaving between my legs, mewing for food. I found some bacon and eggs.

'Shall I make you some?' I asked.

Maggie shuddered. 'I never touch breakfast. Anyway, I'm getting disgustingly fat. I've put on a stone since I married Jack – boredom, I suppose.'

'Where's Pendle's mother?' I asked, putting rashers into the frying pan.

'Rose? She never surfaces before lunchtime.'

'Pendle said she was formidable,' I said, 'so I imagined she'd be all tweeds and corrugated hair.'

Maggie laughed. 'She's stunning, isn't she? Gosh, that bacon smells good. While you're making it, you might as well cook some for me.'

I made some coffee and dished the bacon and eggs on to two plates and we took them into the drawing-room.

'How long have you been married?' I asked.

'About two years. It seems ages longer.' She turned her headlight eyes on me. 'Did you know I was going to marry Pendle before I met Jack?'

Suddenly the room seemed to go dark. 'No, I didn't know,' I said.

'Yes. It was funny really. I came up for a holiday when I was only eighteen, and met Pendle and we had a most terrific affair, not just bed, but endless gazing into each other's eyes, and walks in the moonlight, and passionate letters full of quotations. You know how good Pendle is at making things serious. I wanted to get married at once, but again, you know Pendle. He swore he loved me, but he thought we ought to wait six months so we could find somewhere proper to live.

'And then Jack came home from South Africa. His first marriage was on the rocks by then. He was all brown and his hair was bleached almost white, and he seemed to be always laughing and pulling fivers out of his pocket. I came up to see Pendle for the weekend and fell in love with Jack, and we eloped.

'Rose thought it hysterical, but everyone else was livid, particularly Ace. For the first month we holed-up in a little hotel in Ambleside, terrified that Pen would turn up with a hatchet. But, typical don't-lose-your-cool Pendle, he sent us a nice letter and later even a wedding present. I was disappointed. I've always wanted to have men fighting over me. Then Ace's wife was killed in a car crash so the limelight was directed off Jack and me. We all met up at the funeral. Then Ace took this job working for American television and Jack took over the mill.'

I felt sick. I couldn't finish my breakfast. So this was the girl Pendle had loved, who had broken through that icy reserve. Knowing Pendle, he would never forgive her for jilting him and marrying Jack, but if he had forgiven her he must still love her. Why the hell had he brought *me* here?

'Why is their step-brother called Ace?' I asked, in a desperate attempt to change the subject.

'He's really Ivan. "Ace" stems from when they were children. Three boys and a girl, with Jack the youngest. Ace, King – Pendle, Queen – Linn, and Jack, you see. "Ace" stuck as a nickname.'

'What's he like?'

Maggie took one of the photographs down from the desk and handed it to me.

It was a face you would never forget – black-haired, beetle-browed, very deep-set eyes, high cheek-bones like Pendle's, a large aquiline nose, something slightly cruel about the mouth – a tough, haughty, uncompromising face, used to getting its own way.

'I wouldn't like to meet him on a dark night,' I said lightly.

'Oh, I would.' A dreamy expression came over Maggie's face. 'You can't help fancying Ace. He's a cross between Mr. Rochester and Darcy, but there's a kind of gipsy passion about him like Heathcliff.'

'Why is everybody so scared of him?'

Maggie took another of my cigarettes. 'He holds the purse strings. Old Mr. Mulholland realized what a spendthrift Rose was and left all the money to Ace. He's generous, mind you, but nothing could be enough for Rose. He doesn't suffer fools gladly, but he's still wildly attractive.'

'So's Jack,' I said quickly.

Maggie looked at me out of the corner of her eyes.

'Oh, Jack has very taking ways, particularly with other people's girlfriends, and a very good line in smooth talk, just like his mum. But we're hell together, we rat all the time. Now if I were married to Ace it would be different. I wouldn't dare behave horribly. I've always wanted a man I can honour and obey.'

She really shocked me.

'Let's go and get Rose up,' she said. 'She should have finished her exercises by now.'

I took Rose some coffee, and Maggie went on ahead carrying my cigarette. Rose's bedroom, quite unlike the rest of the house, was enchanting. All pink silk and rosebuds. She was fully made-up, wearing a pink negligee and painting her nails.

'Darlings, you shouldn't have bothered. It's terrible to leave you on your own on your first day,' she added to me, 'but those wretched boys have rushed off to look at the mill. Jack's like a little boy with a new toy.'

Maggie pulled a face behind her back.

'They make the most lovely tweeds,' said Rose. 'Not quite my style but the Americans go wild about them. You'll have to get Jack to give you a piece, and have it made up into a skirt when you get back to London.'

The telephone rang, and Maggie rushed off to answer it, but was back in a few seconds.

'Some awful-sounding man for you, Rose,' she said. Rose brightened, pinched one of my cigarettes and the matches and went out, carefully shutting the door behind her.

'It's that ghastly Copeland, Linn's boyfriend,' said Maggie, trying on one of Rose's lipsticks and wiping it off on the counterpane. 'He's always hanging around. I once asked Jack what his childhood was like. He just said, "My mother was always in love." '

We couldn't hear what Rose was saying, but her laugh rang out over and over again.

'Copeland once told her she had a beautiful laugh,' said Maggie sourly, 'and she's been behaving like a hyena ever since.'

'Does she have lots of people after her?' I asked.

'Oh, millions,' said Maggie. 'Seems extraordinary, doesn't it? She must be at least fifty; but I suppose she's only a few years older than Bardot. I hope I have as much fun when I get to her age.'

71

'What does Copeland do?' I said.

'Calls himself a writer, but we've never seen any evidence of it. He was attached to Manchester University, but he gave it up to write full time and pursue Rose.'

I wondered if he was the tall man I'd seen creeping out that morning. I examined Rose's dressing-table. I'd never seen so many bottles. Her knowledge of make-up and skin care must be positively encyclopaedic. In the middle, tucked into a framed photograph of Jack, was a snapshot of a little girl with blonde hair and blue eyes.

'Who's she,' I asked Maggie.

'Lucasta, Jack's child from his first marriage.' said Maggie.

'She's ravishing,' I said, and suddenly, as Maggie's eyes narrowed, I realized I'd put my foot in it.

'Well she certainly doesn't get her looks from her mother,' she said sharply. 'Fay's an old frump. I can't think why Jack ever married her. And Lucasta's so bloody spoilt, she winds Jack round her little finger. She's terribly jealous of me of course.'

'And you're terribly jealous of her,' I thought.

'Does she come over here often?'

'As little as I can help it. She's an absolute menace when she does . . .'

Her outburst, however, was checked by Rose coming back pink with excitement.

'Admiring my beautiful grandchild?' she said, seeing me still holding the photograph. 'Isn't she a poppet? That was dear Professor Copeland,' she went on. 'He's coming to dinner.'

'There's no one to cook,' objected Maggie.

'So there isn't. Never mind. There's buckets of drink and we can always go out. I thought we'd ask Admiral Walker and the Simons and have a little party.'

Maggie, who was gazing through the rain-smeared window at the grey sky and careering leaves, cheered up a bit. 'It's the last one we'll have,' she said. 'You'll have to give up your cakes and ale once Ace arrives.'

'Yes,' said Rose gaily, 'I *must* remember to stop the milk-man tomorrow.'

And although they smoked their way through three packets of my cigarettes and I cooked and washed up lunch and tea and the thought of Pendle and Maggie was never far from my mind, that day was one of the happiest I spent with the Mulhollands. It was like being in the flat with Jane.

I can't say the same of the evening. Pendle and Jack got home about six. Jack looked tired and headed straight for the drinks tray. Pendle kissed Rose, and ruffled – yes, actually ruffled – my hair. He seemed curiously elated.

'I'm sorry we slunk off at the crack of dawn,' he said to me, 'but we've had a marvellous day. Jack's done wonders with the mill. You should be proud of him, Maggie.' He looked at her for the first time.

'Oh I am, I am,' she said.

'Have you been all right?' Jack asked me, pouring himself a tumblerful of whisky and not even bothering to dilute it with water.

'She's been perfect,' said Maggie. 'A walking cigarette machine and endless lovely food appearing on trays.' There was a slight edge to her voice.

Jack smiled and said, 'I expect you've waited on them hand and foot. My mother is the laziest woman in the world, but my wife runs her a close second.' He squeezed Rose's hand as he said this, but the look he directed at Maggie was decidedly unfriendly.

Pendle lit a cigarette. 'People in boiler suits kept rushing up to me,' he said, 'telling me what a great thing Jack's been for the Mill.'

'He spends enough time there,' snapped Maggie.

'At least I get regular meals at the canteen,' said Jack. 'Did you get my blue suit out of the cleaners?'

'No,' said Maggie.

'You've had all bloody day. Did you go down the house and talk to the plumber?'

'No.' Maggie's lashes swept down over half her cheek.

'Well, what the hell have you been doing?'

'Entertaining lovely Pru,' said Maggie, demurely. 'I know what a fan of hers *you* are. We couldn't leave her alone on her first day.'

Jack shot her a murderous look.

'By the way, Lucasta's coming next weekend,' he said.

'Christ,' muttered Maggie, 'that's all we need.'

My blood froze as I looked at Pendle. His pale grey eyes were gleaming. He's enjoying it, I thought. He likes them sniping at each other.

'Professor Copeland and a few people are coming over this evening,' said Rose.

'Oh God!' said Jack, draining his glass of whisky. 'For once I thought we might get an early night.'

I felt very depressed as I went up to change. Then I thought, to hell with it. Where's your fighting spirit? Put on your warpaint and three pairs of false eyelashes, and go out and get him.

I wore a very simple, very short tunic in coffee-coloured crepe, with a wide belt. At least I had a waist to belt, which is more than Maggie had, and I brushed my curls sleek to my head. I was pleased with my appearance. But it might just be the Mulholland's mirrors – they were so dusty one tended to look good in them.

Jack, meeting me in the hall, gave an appreciative whistle.

'You look like a Greek youth,' he said.

'Is that nice or nasty?'

'Nice and extremely disturbing.'

I was pleased that Maggie wore a purple dress obviously bought before she put on weight. She had added black fish-net stockings, yesterday's green belt and jade earrings.

'That looks smart,' mocked Jack. 'It must have shrunk at the cleaners.' Maggie scowled at him.

At that moment the door bell rang. Answering it, Jack found a man from the Inland Revenue, come to talk to Rose about her tax. He was pasty-faced and bald with a few strands of hair combed across his head, like anchovies across a boiled egg.

'It isn't a frightfully convenient moment,' said Jack.

'Of course it is,' said a voice, and the next moment Rose swept down the stairs, poured into a black velvet dress which showed off her lovely figure, with pearls gleaming round her neck and at her ears.'

'Mr. Ramsbotham,' she said, taking both the taxman's hands, 'I'm so sorry I haven't answered your letters, but I've been away. Come in and have an enormous drink, we're just about to have a party, you simply must stay. Jack darling, Mr. Ramsbotham wants a large whisky.' And ignoring Jack's signals of horror, she swept him into the drawing-room and introduced him to the rest of us.

'Hasn't the weather been frightful?' she went on. 'We're thinking of building an ark.'

Mr. Ramsbotham went rather pink and muttered that perhaps he'd better have a private word with Rose as matters were getting rather pressing, and he *was* expected home for supper.

'Nonsense, nonsense,' said Rose airily. 'It's Friday. A man must unwind after a long week. We can't talk about boring tax now. Actually I'm thrilled you dropped in this evening. I know you're a racing man and I just thought you might be able to give us some tips for Newcastle tomorrow. Here's your drink. Thank you, Jack darling.'

One had to hand it to her. Within seconds, Mr. Ramsbotham was totally hypnotized, discussing racing from nose to nose on the sofa.

Jack and Pendle were still talking about the mill. I sipped my drink and talked to Maggie about Pop Music and took another good look at her, sizing up the competition. She had sat down opposite Pendle and kept crossing and re-crossing her legs, so he must be getting a constant suggestion of gleaming white checkered thighs. She looked carnal and hemmed in, and not what mother would call a 'lady', but who wants to be a lady, when they can exude so much animal health in such a dangerously unhealthy way? Unlike Rose, she wasn't at all flirtatious, she didn't flutter her eyelashes or flaunt her bosom. She just stared at Pendle with that stripping look. You felt if you'd walked between them it would have burnt you like a laser beam.

'You're not to call me Mrs. Mulholland any more. My name's Rose, and I'm going to call you Arnold,' Rose was saying to Mr. Ramsbotham. 'Jack darling, you're not doing your stuff. Arnold's drink's nearly empty.'

'Oh dear,' said Maggie, scooping up a handful of nuts. 'I was going to go on a diet before Ace came back, wasn't I? I wish I had a small bust like you, Pru. It's so much easier for clothes.' She looked complacently down at her own cleavage.

Bitch, I thought. Perhaps she *does* mind Jack chatting me up after all.

'Do you think he's here for the night?' I muttered to Pendle as Vatman enthusiastically accepted a re-fill.

'Expect so. At least he can dance with Copeland.'

CHAPTER SIX

IT was an odd party. Jack mixed a hell's brew with a brandy base. I was as high as a kite after the first glass. Everyone seemed determined to drink as much as possible, as fast as possible. To wash away the boredom, I suppose. Two hours later, things were really in their stride.

Pendle was behaving impeccably, filling my glass, plying me with drink. But there was no message in his eyes. In Jack's eyes, however, there was too much. He never missed a chance to reach my hand or squeeze me round the waist. Every time I looked up, I seemed to see those dissipated blue eyes smiling at me.

Tinkle, tinkle went the ice in the glasses. Conversation became more extravagant. The ashtrays filled and spilled over. My smile was as brittle as a dried chicken-bone, as I saw the passionate concentration on Pendle's face each time he talked to Maggie. I talked to one of Rose's bridge friends about hats.

Everyone fell over Coleridge and Wordsworth who, bored of barking at the door bell, stretched out in front of the blazing log fire. The room was impossibly hot because Rose, worried that Professor Copeland might not appreciate the chilliness of large English houses, had also turned the central heating up full blast.

The Professor arrived late, and stood in the doorway for a minute with his head held high so that everyone stopped talking and looked at him.

'He likes to make an entrance,' said Maggie.

He was wearing a grey herring bone jacket, a blue denim button-down shirt, a black knitted tie, grey flannel trousers, and a big black velours hat, which he left in the hall. In his middle forties, he was one of those tall thin, craggy Galbrathian American intellectuals with an impossibly slow drawling voice, who one felt ought to have one hip permanently hitched on to a broken column and be rabbiting on about the beauties of ancient civilization. He was also without doubt the man I'd seen creeping out in his stockinged feet that morning.

Almost immediately Rose brought him over to meet me.

'Pru's a writer too,' she said airily, 'so I know you'll get along.'

Professor Copeland concentrated on lighting a revolting pipe, looked at me with hooded eyes, and in a slow drawling voice asked what I was working on at the moment.

I was tempted to say Pendle, then said I was only a copy writer, and at present was wrestling with a tinned peaches campaign.

'Not South African, I hope?'

I stifled a yawn, and shook my head, and Professor Copeland in between puffs went on to say that he'd never met an ad man who didn't yearn to be a real creative writer, and he was 'darn sure' I'd got a half finished 'narvel' in my bottom drawer.

Stifling another yawn, I asked him what he was working on at the moment. He said he was researching a 'narvel', which was set in Africa, which he found ethnically interesting, and what a lonely business writing was, and how he'd given up teaching, because he found it so exhausting to 'carncentrate' on creative writing. And on and on and on. God, he was a monster, as long in inches as he was short on charm. Out of the corner of my eye, I could see Maggie bending over the sofa talking to Pendle. I didn't like the way she was letting her hand trail along the back of his neck.

'What's your novel about?' I said.

Immediately Professor Copeland waved a long finger at me.

'No, no,' he said, crinkling his eyes in what he no doubt thought was a fascinating smile, 'I've had so many good plots pinched in the past. I know you wouldn't do it deliberately,

78

but you'd be bound to talk about it when you get back to London. I know what vultures these advertising men are.'

'I hope you've insured the bit you've already written,' I said crossly.

'Come on, Professor, drink up,' said Jack, managing to top up Copeland's glass and pat my bottom at the same time.

'Well just a small one,' said Copeland. 'Normally, I don't drink, I find it dulls the senses, but I've had an exhausting week, I guess, so I owe myself a little relaxation with wine and charming women.'

It was really Rose's evening. What with Vatman, Admiral Walker, Copeland, and sundry elderly letches vying for her favours, she was well away. She put an old record of Night and Day on the gramophone, and danced around waving her cigarette holder in time to the music and sending a cloud of ash on to the floor.

'Come along Admiral,' she said gaily, 'start the ball rolling.'

The Admiral, who had a red face and a laugh like Basil Brush, whistled through his moustache with excitement, and clutched Rose gingerly as if she was a bag of eggs.

'If I hold you up to my ear, Admiral,' said Rose, fluttering her eyelashes, 'will I be able to hear the sea?'

'God awful old bore,' said Copeland scathingly as the Admiral breathed even faster, 'never stops verbalizing about his darned convoys. I better talk with him later this evening to get some more material. I've got a blimpish character like him in my novel,' and he was off.

Really it was impossible to tear Copeland away from himself for more than a second. Thank God, the record ended, and Rose claimed him for the next dance. Next moment, Vatman had taken the floor. He had removed his jacket to show great sweaty patches under his armpits, and was sweeping one of Rose's bridge friends round like something out of Come Dancing.

I inherited the Admiral, who stood, bristling with rage, watching Copeland and Rose.

'Damn shame Mulholland isn't alive,' he muttered. 'Never have let a pansy like that in here. Nor would young Ace for that matter. When's he coming home?'

'Sometime tomorrow,' I said.

'About time too. Place has gone to rack and ruin since he left. Best of the bunch, you know. Oh Jack's got charm, but he can't really carry his corn, and as for that Pendle, chilly fella; always seems to have given too many pints of blood.'

I knew I ought to defend Pendle, but the Admiral seemed about to have a coronary over Copeland as it was.

'Never have allowed a pansy like that in here,' he muttered again.

'He's writing a book about Africa,' I said.

'Never bin there. Don't want to. Full of blackamores. Can't trust these writer chappies. Just read a biography of Monty. Fella made out he was a homo, damned cheek.'

I tried to distract him with small talk, but it was like trying to amuse a dog tied up outside the supermarket, waiting for its mistress to come out.

Vatman, his bald patch glistening with sweat now, paused in his fishtails and *telemaques* to help himself to some pâté and biscuits on the table. Rose's bridge friend took the opportunity to escape his clutches.

'Where on earth did Rose dig him up?' she said in a horrified whisper.

I left her and the Admiral to it, and went and stood by Pendle.

'*You made me love you, I didn't want to do it,*' sang Al Jolson.

'Are you enjoying yourself?' said Pendle with a slightly twisted smile.

'Surprisingly, yes,' I said. Oh *why* didn't he ask me to dance?

Vatman who was really getting uncorked now was trying to cut in on Copeland and Rose.

'May I personally congratulate the lovely lady of the house on her pâté,' he said, 'and request the pleasure of a dance?'

'In a minute, Arnold,' cried Rose merrily.

Vatman helped himself to more pâté, washed down by several other people's drinks. Pendle and I watched him fascinated. Suddenly there was a gasp of horror behind us. It was Maggie; she had turned green.

'What's the matter?' said Pendle.

'Do you recognize the pâté bowl?' she said faintly.

'It's nearly empty,' I said.

'It belongs to Coleridge and Wordsworth. I forgot to put it down for them. Ramsbum's downed an entire tin of Chappie.'

We all looked at each other in horror, then collapsed in uncontrollable giggles.

'I'd better whisk it away,' said Maggie, wiping her eyes, 'before Ramsbum starts lifting his leg.'

'Gimme gimme what I cry for,' sang Professor Copeland in a pleasant baritone, foxtrotting past with Rose.

'You know you've got the kind of kisses that I'd die for,' sang Rose, smiling up at him.

The Admiral went purple.

God, the poor Admiral, I thought. It's all too much like follow-my-leader. The absent Linn after Copeland, the Admiral after Rose, Jack after me, me after Pendle, Pendle, I dreaded, after Maggie, and Maggie, I imagined, after Ace when he arrived.

I'd had too much to drink. 'Everyone's in love with the wrong people in this house,' I said to Pendle.

He looked at me sharply. 'What on earth do you mean?'

But before I had time to answer, Jack came over and asked me to dance. I wasn't very steady on my feet, but as it was old-fashioned music I was entitled to cling on to him.

'Did you have a meaningful duologue with the Professor?' he asked.

'He's ghastly,' I said. 'The Admiral think's he's a pouf. Do you?'

'No, dear,' said Jack, putting on a camp voice, 'but he helps out if they're busy.'

It wasn't all that funny, but I fell about laughing. Jack's arms tightened round me. 'Christ, you're pretty.'

When the record ended, Maggie got up and put on a Rod Stewart record.

And then she started to dance by herself. The way she slid into the rhythm was unbelievable – jungle, sensual. I quickly looked at Pendle, but his face was turned towards her. He was incredibly still.

'Come on, Pen,' she said softly. 'Come and dance with me.'

In one fluid movement, he got up. He'd never danced with me, but with Maggie he was inspired. I've never seen anything so provocative as the way they moved their hips. Pendle's face was completely deadpan. Undulating there, he looked once again as pale and slim and dangerous as a cobra. I was reminded of the way he had behaved in court.

The rest of us were mesmerized. Only Rose and Copeland continued to resolve noisily in one corner.

Jack lit a cigarette and handed it to me, and then lit one for himself. 'I'm afraid we've just witnessed a chemical reaction,' he said flatly. 'Come and look at the moon.' He took my arm and led me into the hall, where Vatman was on the telephone. 'But Monica I shall be home shortly,' he was saying, 'but there is a lot of paper work to go through.'

Jack took me into the dining-room. He didn't bother to switch on the light. There was no moon outside. It was hidden by pale, luminous clouds scurrying across the sky. The rain had stopped, and the lake gleamed white in the valley.

'Beautiful, isn't it?' said Jack. 'I love this place, even if it is falling to pieces. Maggie hates it. I often feel if I packed in the works and got a job in London, she'd he happier.'

'She's very beautiful,' I said dully.

'Pendle's just wanted her for a long time.' At last it was out in the open. I stood very still.

'But she doesn't want him?'

'Doesn't she?' Jack drew on his cigarette, 'I don't know. She certainly wants him to go on wanting her, which comes to the same thing. He ought to live with her for six months; that would cure him.'

'But I don't understand,' I said miserably. 'Why did he bring me up here?'

'I guess he heard rumours that Maggie and I were having trouble – probably from my mother, who loves stirring things. He knows my weakness for redheads, particularly beautiful ones, and brought you up here as bait. The one thing that drives Maggie mad is my chasing after other women.'

'Then you think Pendle doesn't give a damn for me?' I tried to stop my voice trembling.

'I think you've been dealt a marked card, darling. Whether he likes you or not is immaterial. The only thing he wants is to get Maggie back and he's waited a long time to get her. Beneath that rock-hard exterior there's a heart of stone.' Oh dear, he might have been Rodney talking. 'I'm telling you this because I like you – very much – and I want you to get out before you get in too deep.'

I felt the tears rolling down my cheeks at the futility of the last few months.

'I've made you cry. I'm sorry.'

'It doesn't matter,' I sobbed. 'I'm sorry for you, too. Can I borrow your handkerchief please?' It was silk and smelt of expensive after-shave. I blew my nose noisily.

'I got it all wrong,' I said. 'I thought he was serious because he didn't make a pass at me. People usually do, you see.'

'I'm not surprised,' said Jack, and took me very gently in his arms.

It's strange how unhappiness sparks off a mood of frantic sensuality. Jack was just a handsome man, kissing me because I was miserable. But as I felt those powerful shoulders and the thick hair beneath my fingers, and breathed in his expensive cologne, he suddenly seemed like a God. I kissed him back as though he were the last man on earth.

'Wow!' he said. 'Wow!' and he kissed me again. We were so engrossed we never heard the door open. Suddenly we were flooded in light. We swung round blinking. Jack kept his arms round my shoulders. Towering in the doorway, looking faintly amused, was a man I instantly recognized from his photograph as Ace Mulholland.

'Everyone's playing General Post as usual,' he said. 'Now I really know I'm home.' Jack gave a shout of delight and bounded forward.

'Ace! My God! How marvellous. We were expecting you tomorrow.'

'So I see,' said Ace dryly.

'Rose! Everyone! Ace is back,' Jack shouted down the hall.

Rose gave a muffled shriek and after a few seconds came running downstairs patting her hair. Her dress was on inside out. Goodness knows what she'd been up to.

'For heaven's sake Jack, don't play silly games.' Then she saw Ace and turned pale.

'My God, Ace, how wonderful to see you.'

'So nice to feel wanted,' said Ace dryly.

I couldn't take any more. As I fled upstairs I heard him ask, 'Who's that? For a minute I thought Maggie'd lost weight.'

'Pen's girlfriend,' said Jack. 'She's called Prudence.'

Ace laughed. 'A singularly inappropriate name,' he said.

I was horrified when I looked in the mirror. Crying had streaked my mascara, kissing had smudged my lipstick like a clown. The top buttons of my dress were undone, and my bra strap had slipped down to my elbow. I washed my face and tried to screw up enough courage to go downstairs. I jumped in terror at the knock on the door.

To my amazement it was Pendle.

'Pru,' he said, 'are you okay? Suddenly you disappeared. Ace has arrived a day early and my mother's having hysterics. Come and meet him.'

He took my hand and led me downstairs, stopping on the way to say, 'Sorry I've been uptight. This place always has a devastating effect on me. Thank you for being so sweet.' He squeezed my hand and suddenly kissed me on the cheek.

That threw me. I nearly started crying again. What the hell was going on? Perhaps things were going so well with

Maggie, he could afford to be nice to me. On the other hand it was only Jack's word against his. All that talk about Pendle and Maggie might easily be Jack's method of prising me loose from Pendle!

In the drawing-room I was hailed like a long-lost sister. Conversation was very sticky with everyone trying to conceal the fact that they were half cut. All the guests had evaporated which only served to emphasize the chaos. A battalion of empty bottles stood on the table. Records out of their sleeves lay like a handful of loose change in the corner.

'Pru, darling,' said Rose, pronouncing her words very carefully. 'This is Ace, twenty-four hours early, but no less welcome for that.' Ace got to his feet and shook hands with me, giving no sign that he had already met me in less happy circumstances.

'Come and sit down,' he said, pointing to the big armchair, right away from Jack. Pendle sat on the arm. Maggie and Jack were holding hands on the sofa.

'Why *are* you a day early?' asked Jack.

'The Venezuelan riots were crushed much quicker than anyone thought they would be. There was no point in hanging around, so I flew straight back.'

'How long will you be here?' asked Rose.

'Hard to tell – perhaps indefinitely. The B.B.C. have offered me a news programme.'

'That would mean you'd be in England all the time?' said Rose faintly.

'Yes,' said Ace, with a smile that didn't reach his eyes. 'Then I could keep an eye on you all, couldn't I? How's Lucasta?' he said to Maggie and Jack.

'Oh she's absolutely gorgeous now,' said Maggie enthusiastically. 'We've got her next weekend, so you'll be able to see her.'

She'd certainly changed her tune – not a trace of the wicked step-mother anymore.

'Humbuggery is legal after ninety days at sea,' I muttered.

I could now understand why they were all so wary of him. He was tall – easily the tallest of the three brothers – and

85

even broader than Jack, and his skin was tanned to the colour of old leather. He'd grown a black moustache since the photograph was taken, which made him look not unlike a Venezuelan bandit himself, and he obviously hadn't slept for days. But even exhausted, he was formidable. He was one of those tough, self-assured men who rove round the world in search of truth, always where the action is, watching wars begin and governments fall. Each time he opened his mouth, I expected the *Panorama* signature tune to strike up.

He had a rough, abrupt way of shooting out questions, then listening closely to the answers. I sat in a semi-comatose state as he asked Jack about the mill, Pendle about the Bar and Maggie about the new house – just as if he were conducting a series of short, sharp interviews. Each time Rose chipped in, he brushed her aside. Occasionally his eyes flickered over me. My turn would come later. I don't like him, I decided. He's a bully.

Rose picked petulantly at her nail polish for a few minutes, then announced she was off to bed. I went too. In the hall we found someone had left the telephone off the hook.

'What a frightful waste of electricity,' said Rose, putting it back.

This time when I got upstairs, I strewed my clothes all over the bedroom, and when I lay down the room went round and round.

CHAPTER SEVEN

I DREAMT I was trapped by falling masonry, with the flames flickering towards me. I woke up pouring with sweat to find Coleridge lying heavily across my legs. After yesterday's deluge, the waterfall outside the window was thundering on the rocks, which did nothing to alleviate my excruciating hangover. I lay for a bit trying to adjust to the pain. After all, people learnt to live with suffering, people with cancer, and Odette Churchhill having her fingernails pulled out. Just relax into it, I told myself, clutching my head. I gave a low moan. It was no good, I got up and staggered down the passage to the bathroom, where I was confronted by the most glorious back view : broad brown shoulders, thick black hair curling into the nape of the neck, powerful haunches wrapped in a scarlet towel, and long brown muscular legs. Perhaps I'd died after all and gone to heaven.

Next moment my illusions were shattered. Ace Mulholland turned round, the bottom half of his face covered with lather. Under the black thatch of hair, his eyes were swollen with sleep and not particularly friendly.

'Won't be long,' he said, starting to scrape off the soap.

'At least the rain's stopped,' I said faintly, hanging on to the door handle for support. 'We might get a lovely day.'

Then I remembered I was wearing my black temptress see-through nightie, which must look pretty incongruous in my present state of collapse, so I went back to my room, and sat on my bed groaning. If I didn't get a drink pretty soon the top of my head would come off. I put on a brown sweater, and a pair of brown corduroy jodhpurs which were fashionable that autumn. (I'd never been on a horse in my life.) It took centuries to get dressed, and I had awful trouble with my new walking shoes. Every time I bent down to do up the laces, I was nearly sick. It was a bit late anyway to try and impress Ace with my respectability. I threw my walking shoes in the corner, and put on my orange boots. I seemed to have gone downhill rather fast in the last two days.

Clinging on to the banisters, holding my head in place with my left hand, I found Ace prowling round the downstairs rooms drinking black coffee, and looking bootfaced. Certainly the state of decay looked even worse by daylight. Coleridge, now stretched out in the hall, thumped his tail.

'Oh please don't,' I groaned. 'Have you got any Alka-Seltzer?'

'You'll never keep it down in that condition,' he said. 'I'll get you a Fernet Branca.'

In the kitchen I found Mrs. Braddock noisily washing up, trembling with rage that she'd been caught on the hop.

'Mrs. Mulholland should have warned me Mr. Ace was coming back,' she grumbled.

'She didn't know,' I said, remembering Rose's inside-out dress. 'She was more surprised than anyone.'

'Probably never read Mr. Ace's letter properly, and I was going to take the budgie in for a check-up this morning,' said Mrs. Braddock, viciously crashing a saucepan down on the draining-board, which didn't really help matters.

Ace came in with a glass.

I gulped it down, then choked.

'You've poisoned me,' I croaked.

For a second I thought I was going to explode. Then suddenly it was a horror film in reverse. The terrified creature being torn apart by Dracula's teeth was transformed into the radiant bride again. Suddenly I was all right. I shook my head three times. It didn't even hurt.

'Very clever,' I muttered.

Ace regarded me thoughtfully; then, waiting until Mrs. Braddock had stumped off to collect some more glasses, said, 'Do you always drink as much as this?'

I looked him straight in the eyes. 'No,' I said, 'I've been corrupted by your family.'

He sighed. 'I was afraid you had.'

'Where is everyone?'

'Still asleep. Before you came down, I discovered a man from the tax office stretched out in the broom cupboard.'

I giggled. 'He had a heavenly time last night.'

'Well he wasn't feeling so hot this morning, but was coherent enough before he left to give me a few details about the financial set-up here. I'll have to have a session with my step-mother later.'

'Oh dear. Can't you wait till tomorrow? I don't imagine she'll be quite up to it today. I thought you'd sleep in too.'

'I haven't got used to the time yet.'

Coleridge wandered in, gazed at me with lustrous brown eyes, then put a large speckled paw on my knee.

'If he tells you he hasn't had a mouthful since yesterday, he's lying,' said Ace. 'I've just fed him.'

'He's terribly nice,' I said, scratching him behind the ears. 'Where's Wordsworth?'

'Buggered off somewhere, probably after a bitch in the village.'

'You haven't possibly got a cigarette, have you,' I said. 'I left mine upstairs.'

'No,' said Ace, 'You'd do better with some fresh air. D'you want to come and look around outside?'

'All right,' I said. After all it *was* important to get on with Pendle's family, although I'd been getting on a bit too well with Jack.

Ace got me one of Rose's old sheepskin coats from behind the door, picked up a large parcel on the dresser and we went out of the back door.

The most radiant morning greeted us. The air was as soft as primroses. The sun had broken through. Everything in the drenched garden sparkled. Deep puddles reflected a sky as blue as the Angel Islington in Monopoly.

We walked through the kitchen garden, past over-grown gooseberry bushes, blue and green cabbages, full of fat rain drops, and ancient fruit trees, the ground beneath them covered with rotting yellow apples that no one had bothered to pick. Along the fence the remnants of former shrubberies were thickly choked with weeds. There was a lovely smell of wet earth and mouldering vegetation. A robin perched on a spade, thrusting out its orange breast in the sunshine.

At the top of the garden, we went through a rusty iron gate into open fields. At the end of the fields, beyond a belt of dark pine trees, a huge mountain reared up, covered in rocks, khaki grass, and bracken so red it looked as though it had been dipped in henna. Coleridge charged on ahead, snorting down rabbit holes, his plumy tail going all the time. It was very quiet; all you could hear was the occasional mournful bleat of a sheep, and the full roar of hundreds of little becks coming off the mountain.

'How much of the land is yours?' I said.

'About twenty thousand acres,' said Ace. 'Most of it is let to local farmers. It stretches to beyond the village over there.'

He pointed to a clump of little grey houses in the distance. The smoke was going straight up from the chimneys, the sun caught the gold lichened roofs, and the blue dress of a woman who was hanging out washing.

'It's so beautiful,' I breathed. 'Aren't you glad to be back?'

'Not sure yet. Haven't been here long enough.'

Suddenly I decided I rather liked him. Then he started grilling me, and I decided I didn't. It was just like being interviewed for a job. How long had I known Pendle? Where did my family live? What did my father do? How many brothers and sisters had I got? Why hadn't I gone to university? How long had I been in my present job?

'Two years,' I said defiantly – that should show him I'd got staying power. 'If you've got a good job, you hang on to it at the moment. Everyone's nervous. The advertisers are still pulling back. The bosses spend more time worrying about cashflow than producing ads.'

'What do you do?'

'I work for the creative director – and doesn't he create sometimes!'

Ace was like Pendle, he didn't laugh at my jokes either. In need of light relief I kicked a toadstool, and then did a handstand. Coleridge had reached a little stream, and was splashing up it, snapping at the waterfalls.

'He's what they call a "watter" dog round here,' said Ace. 'When he gets home, he'll rush upstairs, and dry off in someone's bed. You'd better keep your door locked.'

I told him about Pendle's rape case.

'Yeah, he did well. I got the cuttings in the States.'

Even abroad he kept tabs on them.

Then he started quizzing me about the English political scene, which was totally disastrous. I couldn't even remember who was Minister of Labour, let alone Shadow Chancellor, and I'd never known what the balance of payments was anyway.

'I'm not interested in politics,' I said crossly. 'They're always changing. Can't we have a commercial break? I really don't care about the State of the Nation at this hour of the morning.'

The dark searching eyes held mine for a minute.

'Do you ever?' he said dismissively.

'Not if I can help it. You should try Professor Copeland if you want serious conversation,' I snapped, and did a couple of cartwheels, which didn't do my head any good either.

We had come full circle now. The house was visible over the hill. We passed a thick clump of silver birches, and reached the stables, and whatever state of delapidation the rest of the house had fallen into, you couldn't fault them. Everything had been newly painted a glossy duck-egg blue, the yard was swept, and the horses in the boxes were in magnificent condition. And one felt that never in the past two years had they ever been anything else. There was also no doubt about the incredulous delight on old Mr. Braddock's face when he saw Ace who handed him the parcel he was carrying. He was too shy to open his present in front of us, but stumped off bowlegged to leave it in the tackroom, and then took us on a tour of the horses.

'This is new,' said Ace, stopping in front of a handsome chestnut, looking balefully out of her box, and pawing at the straw.

'Mr. Jack bought her for young Mrs. Mulholland last summer,' said Mr. Braddock. 'Jumps anything you can see the sky over, but she doesn't get enough exercise.'

We went out to the paddock to look at the ponies. A plump blue roan came bustling up to us, whickering through her nostrils, nudging at Ace with her roman nose.

'This is Bluebell,' he said, pulling gently at her ears. 'She taught us all to ride. God knows how old she is now.'

I was just bending down to pick her some grass, when a pair of hands grabbed me round the waist. I let out a piercing shriek and leapt forward. Bluebell tossed up her head and cantered away.

'What the bloody hell?' snapped Ace.

It was Jack, his hair lifting in the breeze, wearing a dark blue sweater, and ludicrously tight jeans. Even a hangover couldn't dim his beauty.

'Hullo, my darlings,' he said. 'You're up revoltingly early. Aren't you pleased with the horses?' he added to Ace. 'They're all in good nick, aren't they?'

Ace nodded. 'Makes a nice change from everything else.'

'What d'you think of the mare I bought Maggie?'

'Too fat,' said Ace.

Jack laughed. 'Like her mistress, and quite unlike this heavenly creature who's not got an ounce of spare flesh on her. How are you this morning, angel?' He went on grabbing me round the waist again, and pulling me against him. Ace was glaring at us so fiercely, I decided I wanted to irritate him.

'All the better for seeing you,' I said, smiling up at Jack.

'It's nearly opening time,' he said. 'Mustn't give my hangover time to get a grip. Who's coming down to the pub?'

'Oh I am, please,' I said.

'No thanks,' said Ace. 'And for God's sake don't pour too much drink down her. I've only just sobered her up.'

And, turning abruptly on his heel, he walked back to the stables.

We had a nice time at the pub, where we found Wordsworth parked outside, and the Admiral on a bar stool inside, both looking equally lovelorn and the worse for wear.

'Wordsworth's been here all morning whining for our Sarah,' said the landlord, shaking his head. 'Must have got her bad.'

'Know how he feels,' sighed the Admiral. 'How's yer mother this morning?'

'Well she hadn't surfaced by the time I left,' said Jack. 'No doubt she'll emerge radiant at lunchtime. She's got more stamina than any of us.'

'Wonderful woman,' sighed the Admiral. 'What are you going to drink?'

After that we had several drinks, and a post mortem on the party last night, most of which was devoted to in-depth bitching about the Professor.

'He's the most boring man I've ever met,' said Jack. 'And what's more he wears the most boring trousers.'

'Suppose he's very brainy,' said the Admiral, gloomily.

'Second in British English, fourth in life,' said Jack. 'You'll have to go in and fight for her, Admiral.'

The Admiral looked rather excited and bought us more drinks.

Jack and I were exchanging so many eye-meets now it was getting ridiculous.

'We really ought to go,' I said. 'It's twenty to two.'

Dragging a reluctant, panting Wordsworth, we got back into the car, dropped the Admiral off at his cottage on the edge of the lake, and set off for home.

'Gather ye rose buds while ye may, there's no more bed once you're dead,' said Jack. He put his hand on my thigh.

'Wordsworth will be shocked,' I said, removing it.

'He's far too busy composing Tintern Abbey,' said Jack.

I giggled. He put his hand back. I put my hand firmly on top of his to stop it moving further upwards. We were nearly at the bottom of the drive.

'I don't think Ace approves of me,' I said, more to get Jack off the subject of me than anything else.

'Don't think he approves of anything very much at the moment. Must be hell coming back here, with Elizabeth

93

buried in the churchyard, and every tree and rock reminding him of her. She was so lovely, and he adored her so much. He's missed out on love really, with his mother dying when he was only two, then losing Elizabeth *and* the baby after such a short time. I know he's not easy, but he's rewarding if you make the effort.'

He took his hand from my thigh to swing the car in through the drive.

'But where were we,' he went on, 'when Ace so rudely interrupted us last night? I must say I did enjoy it.'

'Oh so did I.' I said. I shouldn't have encouraged him. But he was so attractive, and I didn't think he'd try anything when we were so nearly home.

He stopped the car at the front, smiled at me gently, then in full view of the drawing-room window, leant over and kissed me very hard, full on the mouth which was still half open. For a moment I was too surprised to move, then I pulled away and leapt out of the car. Laughing, quite undisturbed, Jack started up and drove round to the garage at the back.

Pendle and Maggie were talking conspiratorially in the drawing-room when I went in. They gave no evidence of having seen us arrive.

'Rose was ringing up all her friends telling them how ghastly it was to have Ace back and he walked in in the middle,' said Maggie. She was wearing too much rouge, and there was make-up on her white shirt, but she looked sexy enough in a rumpled way.

'I hear you've been round the estate, and visited the pub,' said Pendle, pouring me a glass of wine, 'so you know all there is to know about the area?'

'I had such a hangover, the hair of the dog was the only answer,' I explained hastily. 'The Admiral was in the pub. He's very disconsolate.'

'Professor Copeland's not too happy either,' said Maggie. 'He's already rung up Rose and said he was "mightily annoyed" about the high-handed way Ace ordered him out of the house last night. He wants an apology.'

94

'He won't get one,' said Pendle.

At that moment Rose swept in, looking a bit pale, but with plenty of the old dash about her.

'Hullo, Pru darling,' she said. 'Do you know, Maggie, Snelgroves have refused to send me that silver fox on appro.'

'Not surprised,' said Maggie. 'Considering you kept the last one six months, and sent it back ripped and with toffee papers in the pocket.'

But Rose's butterfly mind had flitted to other problems.

'Promise not to leave me alone for a minute with Ace,' she said, lowering her voice. 'I know he wants to talk about money. I don't expect I shall ever see dear Professor Copeland again. Ace has been so rude to him. I've got nothing to look forward to now except decay,' she added dramatically.

'Never mind,' said Jack, coming through the door, wearing Copeland's hat. 'You've got plenty more beaux to your string.'

Everyone groaned.

Jack admired himself in the mirror.

'Do I look like an intellectual?' he said, crinkling his eyes.

'Take more than a hat,' said Maggie nastily.

'Oh go and play in the traffic,' snapped Jack. He took off the hat, and put it on Coleridge, who was sprawled in an arm chair and took absolutely no notice.

'He's exhausted,' said Pendle, 'after spending five minutes on his narvel.'

Even Rose giggled.

'Ace and I are going to ride after lunch,' said Jack. 'I suppose there will be lunch?' he added to Rose, 'And Pru's coming with me.'

I opened my mouth to protest.

Pendle glanced at my corduroy jodhpurs, 'Of course, she is,' he said. 'She's already dressed. I'll come and see you off.'

Worse still, they all decided to come and see us off. Any courage given me by the whisky in the pub evaporated over lunch, but I still didn't dare tell them I couldn't ride.

We all trooped down to the stables. Three huge horses were led out.

My teeth were chattering with fear. 'Cold today isn't it?' I said to Ace.

Mr. Braddock led the large grey towards me. 'She's called Snowball,' he said. Jack and Ace were already mounted. Rose, Maggie, Pendle, two dogs, Antonia Fraser sitting on the stable roof, blinking her yellow eyes, and a man carting manure were all watching me. I seized the reins and put my foot in the stirrup. Snowball, recognizing a phoney, started waltzing round. I hopped after her.

'I'll give you a leg up,' said Pendle, hoisting me into the saddle. London from the top of the Post Office tower couldn't have seemed further away than the ground. Incapable of standing still, Snowball started to walk sideways and, no sooner had Pendle let go of her reins than she set off at a brisk trot out of the yard into the fields.

'Hey, wait a minute,' shouted Ace. Snowball trotted even faster. Up down, up down, I tried desperately to rise in the saddle, but I kept getting out of time and going bump bump instead.

'Pull her up,' yelled Jack, but in spite of my frenzied tugs, she trotted even faster, breaking into a brisk canter as Ace tried to overtake. Oh, God, a different rhythm – one, two, three, one, two, three. By the time I'd got adjusted to it, I'd lost both stirrups and the reins and was clinging on to her mane for grim death.

Suddenly she plunged her head down in a terrifying grave-yard cough, shaking me to the roots of my foundations then jerked her head upwards and hit me smartly on the nose.

Through streaming eyes, I abandoned all hope as she dived into a little copse of trees. There were branches everywhere.

'Duck your head,' shouted Ace. Out of the copse, into another green field, downhill this time, towards the lake. I was just wondering if a soft piece of grass might be preferable to this bumping hell, when Ace drew even, caught Snowball's rein and pulled her to a jolting standstill.

'You bloody little fool, saying you could ride,' he swore at me. 'You might have been killed by those branches.'

I was on the verge of tears.

'Beastly, lousy horse,' I said. 'How can I steer it when it's all I can do to stay on?'

Ace's lips twitched.

Jack cantered up, laughing so much he couldn't speak at first.

'Darling, darling Pru,' he said. 'You've no idea how enchanting you looked from the back.' He wiped his eyes.

I preserved my wounded dignity for a few minutes and then my sense of humour reasserted itself. I began to giggle.

They took it very gently after that, riding on either side of me like police horses bringing in the Grand National winner. We rode round the lake. A few sheep with russet bottoms looked at us curiously. A water skier clad in black rubber was zipping across the water. Gradually my nervousness disappeared and I began to enjoy myself.

About a quarter of a mile from home, I felt Jack stiffen beside me. Two figures were walking by the lake. No one could mistake that brilliant red hair. The man was obviously Pendle. They moved slowly as people do who have no destination except each other. Pendle picked up a pebble and started playing ducks and drakes. Maggie tried to do the same, but every time her stone just fell at her feet. I saw Pendle put his hand over hers and show her how to flick her wrist. She gave a cry of joy as the stone bounded across the water.

I felt quite sick as Pendle then put an arm through hers and they turned away from us to walk along the lake.

Ace looked like a thundercloud, but Jack merely smiled and rode his horse closer to mine, so our legs brushed.

'Poor idiot, poor besotted idiot,' he said scathingly. 'He never gives up, does he?'

We rode straight back to the stables after that, no one saying a word.

Jack and Ace went off to have a look at Jack's house. I curled up with a book in front of the fire, but fell asleep.

97

I was woken at dusk by Pendle.

'Are you all right, not too bored?' he said.

'I'm fine,' I said, stretching a little, and bending a glance in his direction intended to be subtly wanton.

Pendle gave one of my curls a little tug of endearment.

'My spies tell me Jack's very smitten,' he said softly.

Which spies, I wondered. Ace? Maggie? Rose? Probably all three.

'Oh well, he's very handsome and all that.' I paused in the hope that I might get Pendle worried. 'But I don't think my happiness lies in that direction. Besides, he's married.'

We locked looks for a minute.

Pendle dropped his eyes first.

'About tonight,' he said.

'Yes,' I said, brightening. Perhaps at last he was going to steal down the passage.

'There's a pretty tedious cocktail party on the other side of the lake with fireworks for some reason. Then we thought we'd go and have dinner in Ambleside. There's a new French restaurant opened there. Would that amuse you?'

I took a deep breath. 'I'd much rather be with you,' I said. 'Couldn't we skip the party and go out on our own without the others?'

'Can't really desert Ace on his first night. I think he's a bit depressed, jet lag and all that.'

'It's him that's doing the depressing,' I said crossly. 'Why doesn't he go to bed?'

'Hush,' said Pendle. 'That's not like you.'

'I don't know what's like me anymore,' I said with a sob.

I moved closer, close enough for him to take me in his arms, and kiss me very gently on the lips. I kept my mouth shut – terrified after being asleep all afternoon I might taste horrible – but I felt myself turn to jelly. Then just at that moment Ace and Jack came through the french windows, and Pendle let me go. I nearly wept with frustration. With a shiver, I wondered if Pendle had seen them coming up the garden and just kissed me in order to kid Ace he wasn't running after Maggie.

CHAPTER EIGHT

As I changed for the firework party, I decided to switch tactics. So far I'd played it cool with Pendle. Now for the first time, I decided to show him I was really keen.

My green culotte dress was a show-stopper. I wondered, as I wriggled into it, if it were a bit much for the country. It clings everywhere and has cut-away sleeves and huge cut-outs back and front.

Oh, well, I thought, if it doesn't stir Pendle to frenzies of lust, at least it will annoy Ace.

The Mulhollands' reactions to the outfit were varied and typical. Jack choked over his drink. Pendle didn't bat an eyelid. Rose said, 'I wonder if I could get away with that?' Ace raised a disapproving eyebrow and said I appeared to have run out of material. Maggie walked round and round me and said, 'Oh, what heaven, but how do you go to the loo?'

As we were leaving, mindful of my new plan of campaign, I seized Pendle's hand. 'Can we go in your car, just the two of us?'

Pendle looked surprised. 'Yes, of course,' he said.

It was dark now, but I could still see a ghostly gleam of the lake through the trees.

'It's so lovely,' I said, turning towards him. 'Oh, Pendle, thank you for bringing me up here. I'm having such a wonderful time.'

He gave that watchful half-smile. 'Are you really enjoying it?'

'Oh, I am!' I couldn't resist putting my hand on his knee and leaning over to kiss him.

He didn't flinch – he just drew away from me. I shrank

99

back to my side of the car, feeling just about as wanted as a Christmas Tree on Twelfth Night.

'Sorry, but it's dangerous on these roads,' he said coolly. The hot fever of mortification had not subsided by the time we reached the party. It was a curiously fossilized affair – a few young people, but mostly old women roaring around on crutches, and so many retired colonels that even the flower arrangements were standing to attention.

Rose arrived grumbling because Ace had refused to close all the windows and had put her false eyelashes in jeopardy. She was also annoyed that Maggie had appropriated the Professor's hat and insisted on keeping it on. Maggie and Jack promptly parted like the Red Sea.

Sick at heart from Pendle's rebuff, I flirted outrageously with Jack, who was only too willing to oblige. In a blue shirt that matched his eyes, he was easily the handsomest man in the room and I, if not the prettiest, was certainly the most outrageously dressed. Those colonels couldn't keep their monocles off my bare tummy. 'I'm fast becoming a navel specialist,' Jack told everyone. With everyone else in wool dresses, I felt rather like a street lamp left on during the day.

Maggie and Pendle seemed to have disappeared somewhere and I found Jack's presence curiously reassuring. We leant against the wall together.

'I like large parties, don't you? They're so intimate,' said Jack. 'Look at Ace. Talk about the stag at bay!' I looked across the room. Ace had been cornered by the daughter of the house.

'He's a handsome sod, isn't he?' said Jack. 'Don't you find him attractive?'

Ace looked up and glared across at us.

'No, I don't!' I said crossly. 'He makes me feel I'm in the Upper Fourth, and covered with ink.'

Ace was obviously coming over to break us up. I was dying to go to the loo, so I sloped off to the downstairs cloakroom. Maggie was right, the only thing to do was to take my dress off altogether. I laid it on the floor. In the pile of *Esquires* on the window ledge, I found a story by Graham Greene which I hadn't read. I settled down with enjoyment. The only snag was that I hadn't locked the door properly. A few minutes later it was pushed open. And there I was naked to my enemy with Old Overkill glowering down at me. I gave a scream and snatched the dress round me.

'Jesus,' said Ace.

'Get out,' I yelled.

Ace slammed the door.

Oh, the embarrassment. Still, if he'd flipped through *Esquire*, he'd have seen lots of girls just as naked as me, if not in such an undignified position. Do him good, boring old prig. All the same, it was several minutes before I could screw up enough courage to go back to the party.

Thank goodness the fireworks were about to start, and I could hide my blushes in the garden. Jack brought my drink out to me. Touching shoulders, we watched the fireworks explode over the lake in a blaze of coloured stars, while everyone ooh-ed and ah-ed. Suddenly someone let off a squib behind me and I jumped straight into Jack's arms. He seemed in no hurry to let go of me until he saw the expression on Ace's face.

As soon as the last rocket had emptied its splendour into the night, the Mulhollands made leaving noises.

'Won't you stay for some spaghetti?' said the daughter of the house, flashing her teeth at Ace.

'No, they won't,' said Rose. 'They've got to go on somewhere else. But I think I'll stay. More my age group,' she added to us. 'Besides, they'll need some help with the washing-up.'

'Washing-up!' snorted Maggie, as soon as Rose was out of earshot. 'She can't wait to slope off and see Copeland.'

We dined in a smart restaurant; deep carpets, and waiters rushing around silently with lighted frying pans. Nothing, however, could have been more flambée than the atmosphere at our table.

Ace and Pendle sat on either side of me opposite Jack and Maggie. I found it sinister the way Maggie and Pendle avoided talking to each other.

Jack kept ordering more wine.

'I'd adore to have snails,' I said.

'Well, I will too,' said Jack. 'Garlic's all right if you both do. What a frightful party,' he went on, unfolding his napkin.

'I didn't notice you making major in-roads into it,' snapped Ace.

'Oh, I had a nice time,' said Jack, winking at me. 'But I was worried about the rest of you.'

Soon they were all tearing the party to shreds.

'The daughter of the house was noticeably taken by you, my dear,' said Jack, grinning at Ace, 'Nice to see you haven't lost your touch.'

I had suddenly developed a fearful sore throat, and found I couldn't eat very much after all. The cold night air knocked me for six when we came out of the hotel. As I wandered towards Pendle's car, desperately trying to walk straight, I was grabbed by the arm.

'You're coming with me,' said Ace.

'I'm going with Pendle and Jack.'

But before I could argue, he opened the car door. 'Get in!' he said coldly. One didn't argue when he used that tone. I lowered the window, however, and as Jack and Pendle came out of the hotel I shouted, 'Help! I'm being kidnapped.'

'I'm running Pru home,' said Ace. 'You two take Maggie.'

'Oh, she was coming with us,' said Jack. 'Cradlesnatcher!' he shouted as we drove off.

My giggle faded away lamely. I reached in my bag for a cigarette. The packet was empty. 'Hell' I said angrily.

'You smoke too much,' said Ace. 'Do up your seat belt.'

'I don't fancy them. I don't like being trapped in cars with strange men.'

'Do it up!'

Bloody Hitler – but he was bigger than me. Sulkily I tried

to shove the seat belt into place. In the end he had to do it for me. I cringed back against the seat so no part of me would touch him.

After a couple of miles, he turned off the road down a cart-track stopping at the edge of the lake. Then he lit a cigarette but didn't offer me one. Out of the corner of my eye I studied his forbidding profile. Perhaps the sight of me naked in the loo had been too much for him, and he was going to run true to Mulholland form and make a pass at me. More likely he was thinking about Elizabeth and that car crash. That must have been why he'd made me wear a seat belt. Suddenly, I felt sorry for him.

'What a heavenly moon.'

'I didn't come here to discuss the moon,' he said. 'I want you to lay off my brother.'

I gaped at him. 'Which one?'

'You know perfectly well which one,' he said harshly. 'Jack's married – leave him alone.'

'He doesn't behave as though he is,' I snapped.

'Of course he doesn't, with you egging him on.'

'Me!' I said in amazement. '*Me* egging *him* on!'

'Yes, *you*. Clinging to him like ivy when I arrived last night, snuggling up to him at the stables, wearing that monstrous dress this evening, and pretending you were scared every time the smallest firework went off.'

'I don't like bangs!' I said, my voice rising.

'I thought you came here with Pendle.'

That went home. 'So did I,' I said.

'You probably know Maggie was Pen's girlfriend before Jack ran off with her. How do you think he feels now? The first time he brings someone else up here, Jack just snaps his fingers and she comes running.'

I wanted to scream at him – to tell him that Pendle hadn't taken any notice of me since we arrived, that he hadn't seen the way Pendle devoured Maggie with his eyes whenever he thought no one was looking. But some peculiar loyalty to Pendle – or was it reluctance to utter out loud what I dreaded? – kept me from saying anything.

'Look,' I said, 'I'm not after your precious brother. He kissed me the other night only because I was there.'

'It makes no difference, I suppose, that he's married? You can behave like that with anyone else you like, but not with Jack! Now are you going to leave him alone?'

'I might and I mightn't.'

Ace exploded. 'You bloody well will!' he said.

I lost my temper. 'You don't understand anything!' I screamed. 'You go about like God Almighty on speech day, like a flaming spare prig at a wedding, ordering everyone around just because, to your eyes, they're behaving badly. You never stop to think why they're behaving like that.'

'Cut it out,' he said sharply. 'You're behaving like a child.'

'This time tomorrow,' I said, my voice shaking, 'I shall have left this beastly place and you'll never be bothered with me again!'

He backed the car out and drove down the road. I was trembling all over, but I was too proud to ask him for a cigarette. When we got home I fled upstairs and buried my face in my pillow and cried and cried. Much later someone knocked on my door – and waited – and then knocked again, but I didn't answer.

I was overcome with dizziness when I got out of bed the next morning. I'm going into a decline, I told myself. I dressed and put on a lot of rouge and huge pair of dark glasses. I found Maggie reading the Sunday papers, still wearing Copeland's hat.

'Hullo,' she said, her eyes avid with curiosity. 'We were worried about you. What on earth did you and Ace get up to?'

'Nothing,' I said quickly. 'I suddenly got a terrible headache.'

'I don't know what's the matter with Ace,' she said. 'He's so sour this morning you could make yoghurt out of him. He's got Rose in the drawing-room going through the bills. I wish I was a fly on the wall.'

'Poor Rose,' I said. 'He does jackboot around, doesn't he?'

'Don't blame him really,' said Maggie. 'Rose hasn't paid a bill since he left, not to mention selling the Romney. Then there's the couple of grand here, and the couple of grand there she's touched him for to do up the kitchen, and the roof and the drawing-room. And you can see how much "doing-up" there's been.'

She picked up a colour supplement and began to flip through it.

'And what about your new house?' I said.

'Oh Jack's paid for most of that, although Rose pretends she has. I wish I could work up some enthusiasm about it.'

She went over to the window. 'Jack and Pendle've taken the boat out. I think I might ride this afternoon. Jack's got to work.'

Next moment Rose came out of the study, looking red-eyed. 'Tell Mrs. Braddock I don't want any lunch,' she said faintly, and ran upstairs.

A minute later we heard the telephone click.

'Straight on to Copeland,' said Maggie. 'A thin lot of good he'll be to her.'

But in ten minutes we saw Rose flash past the door in dark glasses and a huge blond fur coat. The front door slammed and there was a scrunch on the gravel as the car drove off.

Lunch was a nightmare – I kept going into a cold sweat and I couldn't eat a thing. Fortunately they were all arguing too heatedly to notice me.

After much bickering, Pendle was persuaded to go riding.

'What about Pru?' said Maggie.

'There aren't enough horses,' I said quickly.

'She's so light she can ride one of the ponies,' said Ace.

'She'd be happier curled up in front of the fire helping me write this damned report,' said Jack.

Ace's eyes were boring into me.

'I'd like to ride,' I said firmly.

'I think you'll find this one easier than the one you had yesterday,' said Ace later, as he gave me a leg up.

He reached forward and took off my dark glasses. 'Don't ride in those,' he said, putting them in his pocket. 'It's dangerous if you fall off.' He looked at me closer. 'You look terrible. Are you all right?'

'I'll get by,' I said coldly.

Maggie – contrary to her normal lethargy – rode like a gipsy. She thought nothing of slithering down a ravine or clearing a five-foot wall.

It was a beautiful day, but great black clouds were massing ominously on the horizon and a chill wind was ruffling the lake. Above us on the mountains sheep were wending their way along the ancient tracks.

About half a mile from home we entered a long grassy ride. Suddenly, Maggie dug her heels into the chestnut.

'Come on, Pen,' she shrieked. 'Race me to the end.' She got a good start, but Pendle immediately thundered after her. Ace was cantering easily and even my pony trundled along furiously.

Maggie was still whooping herself into the lead, but Pendle, using his whip now, was gaining on her. His horse's coat turned black with sweat. A wall loomed in the distance. Maggie was making for a gap, but just as Pendle drew level with her, her horse pecked and she was thrown over its head. She lay in a crumpled heap. Pendle pulled up his horse with such force that it reared round in the air. He was off it like lightning, running to Maggie, his face ashen.

'Maggie,' he said hoarsely, 'Maggie, darling, for God's sake say something! Darling, you can't do this to me.'

Suddenly Maggie opened her eyes and smiled at him sweetly.

'Darling Pen, what a pretty speech. I must pretend to pass out more often.'

Pendle's face twisted with rage. 'God, you bitch!' He slapped her viciously across the face. Maggie gave a moan and burst into tears. Pendle jerked her into his arms and kissed her passionately.

'Pendle,' snarled Ace. 'For Christ's sake!'

Pendle looked up, the fury and defiance in his eyes were

terrifying. 'To hell with you all!' he said. 'She's mine and I love her.'

I'm not built for drama – it was just like a trailer at the cinema. I swung my fat pony round and cantered off the way we'd come, crying great tearing sobs. It started raining and I was soon soaked to the skin. Dusk was falling as I rode up to the house. Jack was standing in the doorway.

'My poor darling,' he said in dismay. 'Ace is out looking for you. Go and get dry. I'll look after the pony for you.'

I dragged myself upstairs. I was feeling really ill. I peeled off my wet clothes and sat on the bed in my bra and pants, my teeth going like castanets.

There was a knock on the door and Ace barged in.

'Where the hell did you get to?' he said.

'Oh, go away,' I said. I swayed as I got up to reach for my dressing-gown.

He caught my arm. 'Sit down,' he said more gently, putting a hand on my forehead.

'I'll be fine in a minute.'

He felt the sheets of my bed and grimaced. 'Damp, of course.' He put my dressing-gown round my shoulders and led me across the passage. 'Get into my bed. At least it's dry.'

I lay down and stared at the photograph beside the bed. This must be Elizabeth. She had a soft, shining face, and masses of cloudy dark hair – no wonder he had loved her.

He came back with a thermometer.

'You can't possibly travel tonight,' he said, when he'd looked at my temperature.

'Stop bullying me!' I snapped, trying to get out of bed.

'See for yourself,' he said, showing me the thermometer. It was nearly a hundred and four.

'Help!' I shrieked, whipping back into bed. 'I'm dying!'

He handed me two pills. 'They'll make you sleep.'

He stood over me till I'd taken them. There was a knock on the door. It was Pendle. His face was grey, but he looked quite calm. Ace left us to it.

Pendle came over and took my hand. 'Sorry you're sick,' he said.

I turned my face away to hide the tears.

'I should never have brought you here,' he said. 'It was a bloody trick, but when you're desperate, you try anything. I *was* attracted by you, Pru, but Maggie's like a drug.'

'I understand,' I said, feeling like St. Teresa on her deathbed.

He looked so haggard I suddenly wanted to comfort him.

'Please take me with you,' I whispered.

'Ace'll look after you,' he said. 'I'll come and pick you up next Friday.'

Those pills must have been killers. He'd only been gone a few minutes when great waves of sleep rolled over me.

CHAPTER NINE

I WOKE next morning back in my own bed and not feeling any better. A fire had been lit in the grate. The smoke made me cough. Ace and Jack came in to see me on their way to the firm's board meeting.

'I've left a note for Mrs. Bruddock to ring the doctor,' said Ace.

Hours later Maggie wandered in. 'I tried to ring the doctor just now but he was engaged. I think he hunts on Monday anyway. Blasted Mrs. Braddock's got flu, too. Do you need anything?'

'I'd love some water,' I said.

She filled the jug from the bathroom. She was wearing a silver-grey silk shirt.

'Isn't it beautiful?' she said. 'Ace brought it me from America. I've been dying to have a gossip with you. Wasn't it awful Pen grabbing me like that? You missed the best part, rushing off. They simply swore at each other after you'd gone. Ace is getting so righteous, he really ought to go into the church.'

'It's only his family being hurt that he minds,' I said. Heavens, who was I to defend him? But Maggie wasn't listening.

'It's incredible this thing Pen has for me,' she said. 'He felt guilty about you. D'you know, he deliberately brought you up here because he knew Jack would fancy you. But I told him not to worry, you were having such fun with Jack. Perhaps we should swap.'

It's a vicious circle, I thought wearily. She droned on until Rose walked in.

'Hullo, sweetie, how are you? Mrs. Braddock's got the bug.

Such a bore – cold meat again for supper. Mustn't come too near; flu can play havoc with one's looks at my age. Are you ready, Maggie?'

'Is it time to go?' said Maggie.

'We're going out, darling,' said Rose to me. 'You'll be all right. They always say starve a fever. We'll be back soon.' She drifted out on a wave of expensive scent.

At first I was glad to be left in peace, but as the hours limped by and night fell, I began to get frightened. One moment I was drenched in icy sweat, the next hot as a volcano. It started to rain and the wind was rising.

The telephone rang. I dragged myself out of bed. Black whirls of giddiness overwhelmed me. It took hours to get along the passage, and as I reached the telephone it stopped ringing.

Burglars, I thought in terror, ringing to see if anyone was in. A door was banging. The wind was rattling the trees against the window pane. I staggered back to bed, delirious with fear.

I don't remember how long I waited, but suddenly another door banged downstairs. Someone was coming up the stairs, moving lightly but inevitably towards me.

'Oh God, Oh God!' I wept.

The door was pushed open. A figure towered in the gloom. I gave a shriek and was about to pull the sheets over my head when I suddenly realized it was Ace.

'I thought you were burglars,' I said, bursting into a wild fit of sobbing.

He crossed the room in an instant and put his arms around me.

'It's all right,' he said.

'I was so frightened.' I sobbed. 'The telephone rang and stopped as soon as I got there.'

'There, there, it's all right.'

He was stroking my hair. I felt sanity flow back into me from the warmth of his body.

'The bloody board meeting dragged on and on. It was me ringing. I came straight back when there was no answer.'

He laid me gently back on the pillows.

'Where's Mrs. Braddock?'

'She's got flu.'

'And Rose and Maggie?'

'They popped out for a minute.'

'For lunch, I suppose. What did the doctor say?'

'He hasn't arrived yet.'

Ace's face blackened. 'He soon will,' he said, stalking out of the room.

I heard him dialling. 'Can I speak to Doctor Wallis? It's Ivan Mulholland.'

There was a pause, then : 'I don't give a bugger if he's in the middle of his supper! I want him over here *at once*.'

Ivan the Terrible! The doctor was over in ten minutes. A little man with spectacles, absolutely gibbering with fear. His hands were cold and sweating when he touched me.

I heard him mutter about pneumonia as he went downstairs. I was scared rigid. I'm a terrible hypochondriac.

'I'm not really ill, am I?' I asked Ace when he came back.

He smiled and pushed my damp hair back from my forehead. 'You'll live,' he said.

'Dear Jane,' I wrote five days later, 'I'm sorry I haven't written before, but my rotten temperature has only just come down. I hope Pendle rang and said I wasn't coming back. His family really are weird. I'd better not say too much as they're quite capable of steaming this open. I wish you were here. Pendle has two brothers. One is terribly handsome and lecherous (right up your street) the other one is older – in his thirties. I loathed him at first, he's very tough and doesn't give an inch, but he's been simply angelic since I've been ill. He brought me a kitten from the stables today to cheer me up. I think Pendle and I are washed up – his choice not mine. I'll tell you about it when I see you. Do write soon. Tons of love, Pru.'

Certainly Ace had been angelic. Never in a million years would I have expected him to display such patience, gentleness and sensitivity; comforting me through the worst phase when I was half delirious and screaming for Pendle, bringing me hot lemon laced with honey and whisky in the middle of the night when I was coughing my guts out. Even on the nightmarish occasion when I forced myself to eat some lunch in an attempt to please him, and promptly brought the whole lot up over newly changed sheets, he didn't bat an eyelid. Afterwards as I sat huddled in a basket, shuddering with mortification, watching him put another lot of sheets on the bed with admirable deftness, I suddenly thought how hopeless Pendle with all his fastidiousness would have been in such a situation.

Not that we didn't have our battles. Ace was inflexible about me taking my medicine, and wearing a dressing-gown, and not smoking, and he promptly confiscated my wireless, when he came in at midnight one evening, and caught me curled up under the blankets at the bottom of the bed, listening to Top Twenty. Nor would he allow me any visitors. I liked that. I didn't feel up to the scrapping and intriguing of the rest of the family. I was quite happy lying in bed, flitting through novels, playing with the kitten, which we christened McGonagall, listening to the gentle snoring of Wordsworth and Coleridge stretched out in front of the fire, and the faint scratch of Ace's fountain pen steadily moving over the notepad. He was finishing a piece on Venezuela for the *Sunday Times* and had holed up in my room, sitting in the big, faded blue velvet armchair, a pile of books and papers at his feet, only leaving occasionally to make telephone calls, or walk the dogs. I admired his application. He could gut a book in three-quarters of an hour, and he only paused occasionally when he was writing to cross out a word, or listen to a few bars of music on the wireless. It was so different from my haphazard methods of producing advertising copy, chain-smoking, gossiping to Rodney, writing endless variations on different bits of paper, only to produce one very undistinguished slogan by the end of the day. Rodney had sent me a bunch of yellow chrysanthemums as big as grapefruit, and a get-well card signed by the rest of the department. All the same, advertising and the tinned peaches campaign seemed very far away. It was very cosy in my bedroom. I got to know the blue and green flower pattern of the curtains extremely well and I found my thoughts straying less and less to Pendle.

Friday was a red letter day. I managed my first meal : chicken soup, hot ginger bread and a cup of tea, and Ace finished his piece as night fell, and went downstairs to telephone his copy through to the paper.

Ten minutes later Jack walked in clutching two enormous whiskies.

'One each,' he said, sitting down on the bed and removing his jacket. 'I thought you might need cheering up, I certainly do.'

'What's the matter?'

'Maggie. She hasn't even got the energy to row with me. She just slops around looking broody.'

'How's work?' I said, taking a slug of whisky. It tasted vile.

'Tough. Plenty of orders, but no one's paying us. My secretary and my wife are both suffering from pre-menstrual tension. My head is splitting from furiously banged doors. They've just opened a home for battered husbands in Manchester. I'm thinking of booking a room.'

I giggled.

Jack edged towards me.

'What's more important, how are *you*? Ace never lets me near you these days.'

'He's looked after me jolly well.'

'The lady-killer with the lamp,' said Jack.

'I'm dying for a cigarette,' I said, 'I haven't had one for nearly a week.'

Jack got out a packet of Rothman's.

'Do you think I dare? Ace'll go bananas if he catches me.'

'Oh he'll be hours yet. It's pretty inflamatory stuff he's phoning through, from the bit I heard downstairs.'

The cigarette tasted fouler than the whisky. I started to cough.

Jack admired Rodney's chrysanthemums.

'Who sent those?'

'My boss.'

'Must have cost a few bob. Is he after you?'

'No – more interested in my flatmate.'

'And who sent that enormous rubber plant?'

I laughed, and coughed even more.

'The Admiral. He wanted an excuse to come and see Rose. He barged in here this afternoon when I was half asleep. Imagine waking up and seeing his bright red colonial face peering through all that tropical vegetation. I thought I was hallucinating. Ace threw him out.'

'Ace is getting much too proprietorial where you're concerned. Not sure I like it.'

I took another tentative puff, and started to choke really badly.

'Oh God, another nail in my coughing.'

Jack patted me on the back. Then his hand slid round my waist, pulling me towards him.

There is a moment when you decide whether or not you're going to have an affair with a man. Pendle was gone. Jack's marriage was in smithereens. He was extraordinarily attractive. We stared at each other for a long, sexy moment. I saw the lines of dissipation creeping round his merry, blue eyes. Not my line of country, I thought. Easy to get, but impossible to hold. He lacks that wintry detachment, that stripped bone quality that attracted me to Pendle.

'You're sweet,' he said. 'All work and no play makes Jack adulterous,' and he leant over to kiss me. At that moment Ace walked in. With a swift glance he took in the clinch, the whisky and my cigarette smouldering in the ashtray. He hit the roof. He absolutely roared at us. I was terrified. Jack edged away from me. Ace grabbed my cigarette, throwing it into the wastepaper basket, and snatched my whisky from my hand, spilling a great deal of it over the kitten, who spat and took it in very bad part.

'Do you want to have a complete set-back?' shouted Ace, his eyes blazing.

'No,' I said nervously, and started to cough again.

'Look at you,' he said. 'Have you got some sort of death wish?'

'She soon will have if you don't stop bullying her,' said Jack. 'Did the *Sunday Times* like your piece?'

'And you can shut up too,' snapped Ace. 'Of all the fucking irresponsible behaviour.'

Fortunately at that moment a diversion was caused by the wastepaper basket bursting merrily into flames.

'Quick,' said Ace. 'Throw your coat over it.'

'Why not your coat?' protested Jack. 'Mine's just come back from the cleaners.'

I started to giggle. Ace grabbed the water jug beside the bed, and emptied it into the wastepaper basket, which flickered and died.

With an effort he gained control of himself.

'I've just been talking to Pendle,' he said. 'He's got a case in Devon that's going to carry over into next week, so he can't make it this weekend. I told him you weren't well enough to travel anyway, so he's leaving it until next weekend.'

It was as though I'd been reprieved. I put it down to the fact I wasn't feeling strong enough to face Pendle.

There was a knock on the door and in walked Maggie. She looked beautiful, but definitely fat. All that misery eating, I suppose. She was wearing a black velvet dress with a cross-laced bodice, but her bust had got so big, the laces were almost horizontal with strain. She was obviously dressed for a party, and had dropped in to show herself off.

'What are you all talking about?' she said.

'Pendle,' said Ace evenly. 'He's not coming up this week-end.'

'What a shame,' said Maggie lightly. (I had a feeling she already knew.) 'How disappointing for you, Pru. Are you ready?' she added turning to Jack.

'What for?' said Jack.

'Felicity's party.'

'Christ. Didn't know she was having a party.'

'I told you twice this morning, but you were so engrossed in your hangover. Are you coming, Ace?'

'No,' said Ace, picking up the empty water jug and going towards the door.

'Oh, do you need a break after all that sick-bed attendance? Felicity'll be frightfully disappointed. I'm sure she's got half Westmorland coming, boasting you'll be there.'

'She'll have to lump it. I never gave her a definite "yes".' He was still extremely tightlipped.

'Oh well,' said Jack, putting on his jacket and draining the remains of his whisky, 'one may as well get drunk at someone else's expense, rather than one's own.'

The front door bell rang.

'Who the hell's that?' said Maggie.

'Probably Vatman,' said Jack.

There were sounds of commotion downstairs. Then we heard feet pounding up the stairs, and a child's voice saying, 'Daddy, where are you?'

'*Jes-us,*' said Jack, 'It's Lucasta, I completely forgot she was coming.'

'Oh God, so did I,' said Maggie in carefully simulated horror.

No you didn't. I thought to myself. One never forgets things one's dreading – like the dentist.

The door burst open, and framed in the doorway, wearing a blond fur coat and jeans, was the most ravishing child. For a moment she stood looking at us – making her entrance, – the image of Rose forty years ago. Then she shouted 'Daddy!' and threw herself into Jack's arms. There was no question of their delight at seeing each other.

'I'm going to be king in the Christmas play, because I'm tall,' she screamed. 'Jason White's going to be Gold, I'm Myrrh, and Damion's going to be Frankenstein.'

Only Maggie didn't join in the laughter.

'And I've got a wobbly tooth,' she went on, opening her mouth and wiggling it for Jack's benefit.

'If you leave it under your pillow, the fairies might bring you 10p,' said Jack.

'The fairies left Jason White 50p last week. You can't get

anything decent with 10p,' said Lucasta, wriggling down off Jack's knee.

'Hullo Lucasta,' said Ace. 'D'you remember me?'

'Of course I do,' said Lucasta, holding up her face to be kissed. 'You used to tell me bedtime stories, without a book. Mummy said you might be here. Did you have a nice time in America? Did you meet Six Million Dollar Woman? D'you know what knocks down little old ladies and pinches their bread?'

'No,' said Ace.

'Bionic Pigeon,' said Lucasta. 'Did you bring me a present?'

'Lucasta,' said Jack in mock horror. 'You're getting even more avaricious than your mother.'

'She said I was to remind you about the school fees. Oh, look at that kitten. Isn't it sweet?'

McGonagall was licking off the whisky and making terrible faces.

'Aren't you going to say hullo to Maggie?' said Jack.

Suddenly all expression was wiped off Lucasta's face. 'Hullo,' she said tonelessly, then turning to Jack, 'Why's she wearing a party dress? Are you going out?'

'Of course not,' said Jack, ignoring Maggie's furious signals. 'Not on your first night. Maggie's wearing a party dress to welcome you. You haven't met Pru either.'

'How do you do,' said Lucasta, sizing me up watchfully. She plainly didn't believe in giving herself too easily. 'Where's Granny?'

'Out I think,' said Jack.

'Is she still going out with James Copeland?' said Lucasta. 'Or has she got a new boyfriend? Mummy says she's a sexy maniac.'

'Your mother's biased,' said Jack. 'Come on, let's go downstairs and find you a Coke, or would you like something stronger?'

'I'd like a highball.'

Jack roared with laughter. Maggie looked like a thundercloud.

Feeling absolutely played out, I lay back on the pillows, and caught Ace watching me. I gave him a beseeching look of apology. For a second he glared at me, then he grinned, his harsh face suddenly illuminated.

'Come on, everybody out,' he said, 'Pru's had enough excitement for one evening.'

'See you tomorrow,' said Lucasta, going towards the door, and adding to Jack, 'If you let me stay up and watch *Bride of Dracula*, I don't mind if you go to that party.'

CHAPTER TEN

NEXT morning Ace went into Carlisle leaving strict instructions that I was to be left alone. The moment he left the house, one member of the family after another trooped in to see me.

Maggie was first, bitching about Lucasta.

'Isn't she a monster? Wouldn't you like to boil her in oil? And do you know what her bloody mother did? Sent me a list of all the clothes she'd put in Lucasta's suitcase, with a letter asking me to tick them off when Lucasta goes home, "because on the pathetic maintenance Jack pays me, I simply can't afford to buy her any more clothes at the moment". The bitch. Alimony is the root of all evil, I suppose.'

Her obsessive rattle against both Lucasta and Fay went on and on and on. You're far more in hate with them than in love with Jack, I thought.

'How's Rose?' I said, trying to distract her.

'Well, she's promised Ace she won't have Professor Copeland in the house anymore. He doesn't approve of her stealing Linn's boyfriend. Probably having him in someone else's house.'

At that moment Rose appeared in the doorway, buckling under carrier bags.

'What *have* you got there?' asked Maggie.

'Oh a few little things, tights and so on,' replied Rose airily. 'I've got to have something new with all the Christmas parties coming up. Actually I bought them yesterday, and hid them in the potting shed. Couldn't wait for Ace to go out so I could smuggle them in. I must say I shall never forgive him for being *so* beastly to poor James, and so rude to me too. I mean, I *am* his mother.'

'Step-mother,' said Maggie bitterly. 'It makes a difference. I shudder to think what life would be like if I was ever dependent on Lucasta.'

'Life's very hard,' said Rose, patting her curls in my mirror. 'I thought James and Ace would get on. I expected them to have so many good talks about books.'

'Ace says Copeland's knowledge comes more from the beginning of books than the end,' said Maggie.

'Ace's always being cynical and sarcastic,' said Rose. 'I expect he's jealous of James. Oh well, if he doesn't want to communicate with one of the keenest minds on Western Civilization, good luck to him.'

Good luck was plainly the last thing she wanted Ace to have.

'Who said James had one of the keenest minds on Western Civilization?' asked Maggie.

'James did,' said Rose simply.

'Oh come *on*,' said Maggie. 'Let's go along to your bedroom and see what you've bought.'

'There's a very exciting offer for garden furniture in the *Mail*,' said Rose.

'When is it warm enough here to sit outside?' said Maggie, as they went towards the door.

God, I felt tired. Without Ace, I was totally defenceless.

'Hullo,' came a voice. 'How's your Ammonia?'

It was Lucasta.

'Better,' I said. 'I might get up and have a bath soon.'

On one arm she was wearing a fluffy puppet fox, with sleepy eyes disappearing into its fur and a long tail.

'He's lovely,' I said.

'Ace brought him back from America. He's called Sylvia; he's my best toy.'

'He looks a bit like your father.'

'Daddy's gone to see the Burrow engineer about the new house. When he moves in, he wants me to come and live with him.'

'That's nice,' I said. That would finish Maggie off altogether.

'Can I have an apple?' she said, making the fox select one from the fruit bowl, and eating on the side of her face to avoid her wobbly tooth.

'I wish it would snow,' she said, 'Every night I pray for snow and it never comes.'

'What else do you pray for?'

Her blue eyes narrowed. Suddenly her little face looked very hard.

'That Maggie might go away and Daddy might marry Mummy again.'

'Oh dear,' I said. 'I wouldn't do that.'

'I hate her,' said Lucasta, 'and she hates me being here. Every time Daddy takes me out she gets cross.'

After a few bites she got bored with the apple and, going to the cupboard, selected a pair of my black high heels and put them on.

'I'm on Book Four,' she said. 'Shall I go and get it?' She teetered off out of the room.

A minute later she teetered back, sat on my bed, and read the whole book through in a high sing-song voice without a single mistake.

'That's brilliant,' I said in surprise. I seemed to remember Maggie saying she wasn't very bright.

Lucasta grinned and shut the book.

'And I can read it without the book too,' she said and proceeded to reel the whole thing off from memory.

I was still laughing, when there was yet another knock on the door. This time it was Mrs. Braddock.

'And how are you, love? Feeling better, I hope. Now come along,' she added to Lucasta, 'you know Mr. Ace said Miss Pru wasn't to be bothered.'

'I'm not bothering her,' answered Lucasta. She turned to me. 'Do you know, Mrs. Braddock can do magic? She did some in the kitchen today . . .'

Mrs. Braddock looked smug and smoothed down her apron, waiting, no doubt, for Lucasta to describe some particularly delicious concoction she'd run up that morning.

'Well what is it?' I said.

Lucasta gave a naughty giggle.

'She can take all her teeth out and put them in again.'

I loved the Mulhollands, I loved them all, but I couldn't cope with them at the moment. I couldn't cope with the feverish cross-currents. I felt like the centre court net at the end of Wimbledon fortnight. All I wanted was to go back to the peace of Ace and me being shut up together. 'It's because I haven't been well,' I kept telling myself.

Mrs. Braddock and Lucasta were shortly followed by Jack, back from the Borough engineer. When he'd finished grumbling about the builders and his hangover, he said, 'Since I'm obviously not allowed to seduce you, or bring you a drink, shall we have a game of chess?'

'All right,' I said. 'That would be fun.'

As we were setting up the board, Maggie wandered in and watched us sourly.

'You never play with me,' she said accusingly to Jack.

'I do,' protested Jack. 'I played with you the other day.'

'Ah yes,' said Maggie bitterly, 'but that was chess.'

On Sunday matters came to a head between the two of them. They had been to a drinks party at midday and carried on drinking through lunch, getting more and more stroppy. I wandered downstairs in the afternoon – it was my first time up. I felt dreadful, so exhausted in fact that I had to hang on to bits of furniture. I found Maggie in the drawing-room with the Sunday papers and a bottle. She had that sulky petulant look of a cat huddling on a window ledge to keep out of the rain.

Outside in the garden Wordsworth was chewing on one of the Sunday joint bones, and Coleridge, who'd already buried his, was walking round and round under the weeping ash tree wiping his face on the twigs. Jack, Ace and Lucasta were making a bonfire. Jack was pulling up undergrowth with the exuberance of too much alcohol, and fooling around with Lucasta. Ace was laughing and breaking up sticks. He was wearing a thick black sweater. I thought what a handsome trio they made, then collapsed on to the sofa wondering if it were possible to feel so weak.

'Have you got Ace's piece on Venezuela?' I said.

'Here,' said Maggie, throwing the Review Section across to me. 'It's the only decent thing in the paper this week.'

They had given him a huge by-line, and a picture, taken before he'd grown a moustache. He looked younger and much less sombre. He wrote very well. The prose was spare and economic, but his powers of observation were amazing. It was as though he had a hundred eyes like Argus. You could feel the heat and dust and despair of the rebels. You felt as though you were there.

'It's terribly good,' I said in surprise.

'I know. And he's just as good on the box. That's why he's being head-hunted so much at the moment. God, I hate the country,' she went on, refilling her glass. 'Nothing to do for days on end, no one to drive me to the sea when I want to go to the sea. Nothing round me except sulky faces, and mine is the sulkiest of all. What shall we do now?'

In the end we settled down together to do a huge jigsaw puzzle of the New Avengers. It was all either of us were fit for. It was nearly dusk when Jack came in.

'Hullo, lovely,' he said to me. 'How are you feeling?'

He was about to ruffle my hair; his hands smelt of wood smoke.

'I wouldn't,' I said. 'Ace won't let me wash it. It's coming off my head. I'm sure I've got scurf.'

'I never get scurf,' said Maggie smugly.

'You're too thick-skinned,' remarked Jack, bending over the puzzle. 'Bags I put in Joanna Lumley's crutch. I'll get it,' he said as the telephone went.

'Darling, how are you,' we could hear him saying from the hall. 'So sorry I missed you the other day. Why didn't you pop in?'

'I think this is a bit of Steed's bowler hat,' said Maggie.

'Who is it?' I whispered.

'Well, we know her name's "Darling",' said Maggie.

'No, she's being marvellous,' Jack went on. 'Kept us all in

fits. She's out with Ace at the moment, flying the kite. He bought her the most fantastic fox puppet back from the States. Yes, he thinks she's terrific.'

Maggie stiffened, and her hand moved slower and slower over the puzzle, ears on elastic. It must be Fay on the other end.

For at least a quarter of an hour Jack had a very leisurely gossip about the family, Copeland, the Admiral, and Pendle having been up for the weekend. I didn't dare look at Maggie. Jack *must* be still tight, or he'd never have made such a meal of it.

I glanced round. He was lounging on the hall chair, his feet up on a table, smiling into the telephone, utterly relaxed.

'When do you want Lucasta back?' he asked eventually.

There was a long pause. Maggie unseeingly shoved a bit of Steed's umbrella into the sky.

'But that's marvellous,' Jack went on enthusiastically. 'That's a real break. I'm *so* pleased for you, darling. Until Thursday? Of course we can. No problem. No don't worry about that; we'll have her birthday party here. We've had enough practice for Christ's sake. You can't possibly organize it if you're working. Maggie's got nothing to do.' Maggie clenched a pile of sky up in her fist. 'And Ace is here, and Pendle's girlfriend Pru. She's been ill, but Lucasta adores her and she'll be on her feet by then, so there's only my dear Mother to rot things up ... You've booked a conjuror? Well tell him to come here instead, we'll pay the petrol ... Of course we will, it'll be fun, don't worry about a thing. If you get away early on Thursday, come to the party. I know Ace'd love to see you ... O.K. then and good luck, darling.'

Maggie got up and poured herself a drink. Her hand was shaking so much she spilt most of it. Her green eyes blazed. She looked like the Queen in Snow White, and as quite as capable of cutting out Lucasta's heart.

Jack wandered into the room, looking pleased with himself.

'Well, well, well,' he said.

It was extremely unwell. I wanted to hide under the sofa.

'I suppose you want a drink,' said Maggie softly.

'You read me like a book,' said Jack. 'Rather a bad one admittedly.'

He was still tight.

'That was Fay,' he went on. 'She's got a small film part at the beginning of next week.'

'Playing the back of the pantomime horse, I suppose,' said Maggie.

'So I said we'd keep Lucasta here.'

'For how long?' These words were dropped like pebbles into a deep, deep pool.

'Until Thursday night. It doesn't matter if she misses school.'

'And who's going to look after her?' said Maggie.

Jack filled his glass. 'Why you are, darling. It'll do both you and Lucasta good to have some time together with me out of the way.'

'I've got things to do. Tomorrow, Tuesday *and* Thursday.'

'Well you'll have to cancel them and think of someone else for a change,' said Jack sharply, picking up the sports page. 'Oh sod it, United lost again.'

'I should have expected it of Fay,' said Maggie belligerently. 'Trust her not to give anyone any warning.'

'She's only just heard about the part,' protested Jack.

'Oh, very likely on a Sunday afternoon! She's just bloody inconsiderate.'

Jack went on reading the paper. 'What have you got against her? She's never done you any harm.'

'Oh yes she has,' hissed Maggie. 'She divorced you. If she hadn't, I'd never be saddled with you now.'

Still Jack didn't look up.

'There's an extraordinary story here,' he said to me, 'about a woman who's trying to get a crossing for toads on the Preston Motorway.'

'Don't bug me,' screamed Maggie. 'It's a pity you're not married to her if you think she's so wonderful.'

'I wish I was,' said Jack quietly.

'Oh no,' I said. 'Don't say that, please don't. You're both pissed. You'll regret it later.'

'You keep out of it,' yelled Maggie. '*You* haven't been behaving like a vestal virgin since you came up here.'

Then the explosion came. Jack threw down the paper and got to his feet. 'You spoilt little bitch,' he said softly. 'You've never done a bloody stroke in your life. You're lousy at housework, you can't hold down a job, you can't organize the builders, or even remember to pick up a suit from the cleaners. The only thing you show any talent for at all is writing cheques, and bitching about my first wife. But you're so bloody jealous of her you can't even be civil to my child.'

'Your child is a monster,' howled Maggie.

'Leave her out of it.'

'How can I? You asked her stay on.'

'It never enters your thick head, I suppose, that if Fay gets work *I* won't have to work so bloody hard to keep her in alimony. But you wouldn't think of that, would you? You're so wrapped up in yourself, you never give a fuck what I do.'

'And I suppose old Fairy Fay did.'

'Yes, she did. She loved me.'

Maggie was very white around the mouth.

'Why did you leave her then?' she screamed.

'Christ knows,' said Jack.

'I'll tell you why. Because you were bored to death with her and she was no good in bed.'

'She was a bloody sight better than you, if you want to know.'

Maggie gave a little gasp.

I put my head in my hands.

'At least she didn't just lie back and think of Pendle,' said Jack viciously.

There are things that couples should only say to each other in bedrooms, when they get a sort of sexual kick out of seeing who can hurl the worst insults, knowing the battle will end up in bed.

'Stop it,' I screamed, 'Stop it.'

Jack took no notice.

'Just for four days out of your useless life,' he went on, 'you've got the opportunity to do something useful, to create some kind of relationship with Lucasta and you reject it.'

'And if I'm lucky,' hissed Maggie, 'I get a conjuror to help me on Thursday. What's all that about? You bastard. So that old bag was better in bed than me was she? And I have to act as Nanny to her flaming child. Well I won't do it.'

'I'll be here,' I said miserably, 'I'll look after her.'

'Oh darling,' said Maggie, turning her fury on me. 'Ace wouldn't hear of *that*. We can't have his precious patient having the tiniest set back.'

'Oh shut up,' I shouted.

The door opened and in came Lucasta.

'Daddy, my tooth's come out, so that's 50p from the fairies, and we lost the kite up a tree. Ace is still trying to get it down.'

'Jesus,' said Jack. 'We're now welcoming world listeners.'

I fled upstairs, trembling. I couldn't bear it. Maggie had said awful things, but Jack had bugged her by that deliberately provocative telephone conversation, and afterwards he'd said far worse things than she had. Matters may have come to a head too. But I could see that their relationship was like a hydra. In a few hours it would have grown a dozen more heads.

I did my teeth and collapsed into bed. Oh the blissful welcome of cool, plumped pillows and smooth, turned-down sheets. The fire had been banked up, the water jug filled, and a new spray of winter jasmin put in the blue vase. All my mess of apple cores, books, tissues and sweet papers had been tidied up. Immediately McGonagall landed in the middle of my stomach, all four paws sticking out, tail going straight up in the air. Next moment he dived under the eiderdown, bicycling furiously against my toes.

I lay back on the pillows, still shaking.

The door opened and Coleridge wandered in, followed by Ace.

'Good girl.' He walked round the bed examining me as

though I was a building site. 'You didn't stay up too long? How do you feel?'

'Fine,' I said brightly.

'Liar.' He put a hand on my forehead, 'What happened?'

'Maggie and Jack had a bit of a row.'

'They were boiling up for it. Might clear the air. What was it about?'

'Fay's got a part. Jack said we'd hang on to Lucasta until Thursday, and have her birthday party here. Maggie had a go at Fay and Lucasta. Jack stuck up for them.'

'A bit too much?'

'Much too much.'

Ace sighed. 'Christ, they never let up, do they? What d'you want for supper?'

'I don't know.'

'How about some smoked salmon, and a glass of champagne?'

'Oh God, that'd be lovely.' Suddenly happy again, I looked at him out of the corner of my eyes. 'Won't that give me a complete set-back?'

Ace laughed. 'Probably. I've given up.'

'I liked your piece,' I said. 'It was wonderful.'

He seemed surprisingly pleased.

'But you must be used to people telling you how good you are.'

Ace shrugged. 'All writers run on flattery; you must know that.'

Coleridge chose that moment to clamber heavily on to the bed, with the kitten swinging for grim death on his tail. Pretending to ignore Ace, Coleridge circled three times then curled up on my feet and closed his eyes with a deep sigh.

'I may have given up,' said Ace, 'but I've still got some standards left. Get off Coleridge.'

He won't be nearly so attractive when his suntan fades, I tried to tell myself.

CHAPTER ELEVEN

AFTER breakfast on Monday morning Lucasta wandered into my room. her eyes brimming with tears.

'My tooth's still there,' she wailed. 'The fairies forgot to come.'

'Oh poor darling,' I said, putting my arms round her.

'And Daddy's gone off to the office without even saying goodbye.'

She sobbed even louder. I suddenly realized how insecure she was, behind the precocity and apparent sophistication.

'What's the matter?' said Ace appearing in the doorway.

'The fairies forgot to come.'

'They're terribly busy at this time of year,' he said, 'helping Father Christmas sort out all the toys. Sometimes they turn up a bit late.'

'Why don't you try again tonight?' I said.

'Keep her here,' Ace mouthed to me over Lucasta's head.

'That's a nice nightie,' I said.

Lucasta sniffed. 'Can I have a sweet?'

'It's a bit early. Would Maggie let you?'

'Oh Maggie doesn't mind what I do,' said Lucasta bitterly. 'She likes me being naughty, then she can grumble to Daddy.'

She unwrapped the lemon sherbet, dropping the paper on the floor.

'Shall I draw you a picture?'

'Why don't you do one for Maggie?'

'I hate her.'

'If you were nicer to her, she might be nicer to you,' I said. 'And Daddy'd be so pleased.'

'Daddy doesn't like her. He's always shouting at her. What's a "slut", by the way?'

'That's enough, Lucasta,' said Ace, coming back again. 'For very special people, the fairies work overtime. Why don't you go and have another look?'

'All right then,' said Lucasta, and scampered off.

'Poor little sod,' said Ace, 'too much spoiling, too little attention. Look, I'm going into Manchester today. The B.B.C. want to see me, and I've got to have dinner with the Granada people tonight. I thought I might as well kill two birds. Will you be all right?'

'Of course I will,' I said quickly. 'Oh, do look at McGonagall.'

The kitten, having pounced on Ace's shoe laces, frenziedly pedalling at them with all paws, suddenly shot up his trouser leg, leaving only a ginger tail sticking out.

'The fairies have come, the fairies have come,' screamed Lucasta, thundering down the passage. 'They've left me 50p. I must go and show Granny.'

'You make a lovely fairy,' I said to Ace, after she'd gone.

'Wish I could magic up some fairy gold to pay a few bills,' said Ace. 'Talk about walking into the valley of Debt.'

It was a relief to joke. I was still dismayed how much I disliked the thought of him going off all day.

'If you don't overdo things,' he said as he was leaving, 'I'll drive you down to the sea tomorrow.'

'Can I wash my hair?' I said.

'No, I'm not risking you catching cold.'

I got up for lunch, still feeling very shaky. I was appalled at my appearance in the mirror. I'd lost pounds, and my hair was hanging round my grey little face like damp seaweed. I couldn't go out with Ace looking like this. I heard voices whispering outside.

'You ask her,' I could hear Rose saying.

'No you ask her,' said Maggie. 'It sounds better coming from you. Anyway she seems to rather like children.'

I opened my door. They were in the passage dressed to go out. I felt so pale and drab beside them.

'Darling,' said Rose, 'Mrs. Braddock's going to Bingo this

afternoon. She's been so grumpy recently, I thought she needed cheering up, and Maggie and I are going out to lunch in Ambleside, so we thought you wouldn't mind looking after Lucasta.'

After lunch Lucasta and I walked down to the village shop to spend her 50p. It was a dull, cloudy day; the lake was as black as satin. Every tree was bare now – December naked. On the way home we walked through the churchyard, sucking humbugs and playing hide and seek behind the tombstones.

'My Aunt Elizabeth's buried over there,' said Lucasta, pointing to a new white tombstone under a willow tree.

'Elizabeth, beloved wife of Ivan Mulholland 1951–1975,' I read. She'd been so young. Only a year older than me. On the grave somebody, probably Ace, had laid a bunch of freesias. Oh God, why did everything make me cry at the moment?

'When you die, God lives you and turns you into a fairy,' said Lucasta.

When we got home we made hot buttered toast in front of the fire and looked at family photographs.

'There's Mummy and Daddy's wedding,' said Lucasta.

I was surprised that Fay was so pretty. From Maggie's descriptions, I'd expected her to be an old frump.

'And there's my christening. Wasn't I a sweet little baby?'

It was a picture of Fay holding Lucasta in long white frilly robes, and Jack looking on fondly and proudly. I hoped Maggie didn't look at these photographs very often. She'd be lacerated with jealousy.

The person I found myself looking at most was Elizabeth, with her cloud of dark hair, and her huge eyes. I noticed how besottedly she smiled up at Ace, and how handsome and young and carefree he'd looked in those days. What wouldn't I give to make him look happy like that again?

Later Lucasta and I were watching television after supper when Rose arrived with Professor Copeland.

'Ace won't be back for hours,' she whispered, coming into the study, 'so we're just going to have a little drink.'

'I'll leave you to it, then,' I said.

'That'd be kind, darling. James is terrified of catching your cold.'

Wearily I went upstairs. I still had cotton wool legs and felt absolutely knackered. I was appalled how much I was missing Ace. Suddenly I caught sight of my awful hair in the landing mirror. I'd never get him that way.

To a counterpoint of Lucasta's chatter, I did my nails, plucked my eyebrows, shaved my legs, and had a bath.

'I really think you ought to go to bed,' I said feebly.

'I'm not tired.'

To hell with Ace; I must wash my hair. I could dry it by the time he got back. Oh, the bliss as the dirt streamed out!

The only socket that fitted the plug of my hairdryer was on the landing under the cuckoo clock. I sat in the passage on a carpet worn almost bare by generations of Mulholland children waiting for the cuckoo to come out. Lucasta wandered off to watch Starsky and Hutch. I'd only just started drying my hair when I felt a tap on my shoulder. I looked round and nearly jumped out of my skin when I saw it was Ace.

'What the bloody hell do you think you're doing?' he snapped, ripping the plug out of the socket.

'Sitting in a nightie with wet hair in howling draught,' I muttered, and fled into my bedroom. Fortunately Mrs. Braddock had lit the fire.

Ace picked up a towel and sat down in the blue velvet chair. 'Come here,' he said. 'It'll dry all fluffy,' I grumbled. I thought he'd rub my head off.

'Now finish it off.'

He sat down on the bed and lit a cigarette. I looked at him under my lashes, as I crouched by the fire. I saw that he was grinning.

'You're impossible,' he said. 'I only have to leave this place for half a day for complete anarchy to break out. Every light blazing, Lucasta watching the sort of television bound to give her nightmares, and my step-mother and the egregious Professor Copeland drinking gin in the drawing-room.'

'Did you throw him out?' I said.

'Couldn't be bothered. Rose was so upset last time. Thought I'd be nice to him for a change.'

The kitten emerged from under the bed and teetered towards him. He scooped it up on to his knee.

'Did you have a nice dinner?' I said.

'Bloody boring.'

'Who was there?'

He reeled of a string of stars.

'You mustn't be so blasé,' I said. 'I'd give anything to meet people like that.'

'They're no more exciting than the fishmonger or the post-man once you get to know them.'

McGonagall was purring like a turbo jet engine, as Ace stroked its blond tummy. Lucky, lucky kitten, I thought involuntarily.

'Will Granada offer you a job?'

'Probably. But still don't know if I want to settle in this country.'

He put the kitten down, and got up and felt my hair.

'You're dry,' he said and, taking my hands, pulled me to my feet. I had an insane feeling he was going to kiss me, but he just said, 'Into bed with you.'

'Can I read?' I said, as I snuggled down under the sheets.

'I suppose so. Not for long.'

'Are you going to bed?' I said.

'I thought I'd go downstairs and try and find out what makes Professor Copeland tick. Monumental egotism, I should think.'

'You're going to bury the hatchet?' I said. 'That's nice.'

'Bury it in his cranium more likely.'

For a minute he looked at me, frowning thoughtfully.

'Funny, I missed you today.'

I felt myself going scarlet.

'Goodness, that's the first nice thing you've ever said to me.'

'You haven't given me much chance,' he said, and was gone.

A fat lot of reading I did after that. He missed me, he actually said he'd missed me. O.K. It was a millionth of what he'd ever felt for Elizabeth, but it was a start.

Next day, after a sleepless night, as I was getting ready to go out, Maggie wandered into my room.

'God, I feel depressed,' she said.

'Why don't you come out with us?' I said, praying she wouldn't accept.

She shook her head. 'I thought I'd go into Manchester and buy a dress. Can you lend me a tenner?'

The next visitor was Lucasta, driving me spare while I was trying to do my face. Could I do her hair in a pony tail? Could she try on my 'lip stick'? Could I do up the sleeve buttons on her shirt?

In a pathetic attempt to appear healthier, I slapped on suntan make-up, and a bright coral lipstick, but it made me look like an old tart, so I washed it off and settled for looking pale and interesting. With my wildly dishevelled curls which were quite out of control as a result of Ace's drying methods, I looked a bit like Swinburne. Certainly I was raring to swop the lilies and languors of virtue for the roses and raptures of vice.

'Why aren't you wearing a bra?' said Lucasta, as I pulled on a dark sweater and jeans.

'Because the only bra I brought needs washing,' I said untruthfully.

'Can I come with you? I promise I won't talk all the time.'

'No you can't,' said Ace from the doorway. 'Pru had to put up with quite enough of you yesterday.'

'Pru's not wearing a bra,' announced Lucasta.

Rose lent me a pale suède coat with a fur lining and hood.

'The forecast says the temperature's going to drop and I don't want you catching cold,' she said, adding out of the corner of her mouth, 'and do keep Ace away as long as possible.'

'I'm sure Professor Copeland is already mewing outside Rose's bedroom waiting to be let in,' said Ace as we drove down the drive.

It was one of those days that seemed to have lingered over from summer. The air was gentle as silk, and everything was suffused in a golden glow.

We had lunch at a little seaside pub and ate shellfish and drank buckets of white wine.

Suddenly I found I was terribly shy with Ace. My conversation kept sticking, then coming out in great dollops like tomato ketchup.

'This is what I call hard core prawn,' I said, spiking a large piece of shell fish. 'I must say it is heavenly to have a day out. Not that I don't love all your family,' I said hastily.

'They drive me demented,' said Ace.

'You shouldn't worry about them so much.'

'I know, and I must stop telling them what to do. If they want to drink and fornicate themselves stupid, it's no concern of mine.'

I giggled. 'Let them fight their own battles. How did you get on with the Professor last night?'

'Awful. He tried to relate to me.'

'You've got enough relations round here as it is.'

Ace grinned. 'He said he wanted to have an in-depth discussion on my piece on Venezuela, because he found so many parallels with his book on Africa.'

'And he was off?'

'Exactly. Three-quarters of an hour of absolute tripe on Botswana. I'm supposed to be trained to cut people off when they started waffling, but Jesus, Copeland had me beat. I don't believe he's written a word of that book either; it's all talk.'

'Poor Rose,' I said, gouging bread along the grooves of my cocquille shell, soaking up the last traces of sauce, 'she needs a nice millionaire in shining armour.'

'She needs a kick up the arse,' said Ace. 'Any millionaire would be bled white in a matter of months. Solvency's a question of attitude not income. She's having a terrible effect on Maggie too. In a way they compete. Maggie sees Rose getting off with half Westmorland, and can't see why she shouldn't do the same. The sooner Jack gets her into that house the better.'

'She ought to have a baby.'

'Of course she should. Give her something to do.'

'Have they been trying?'

'They're being extremely trying at the moment,' said Ace. 'I want to knock their heads together. D'you want some pudding?'

'No thanks. Just coffee. If she had her own baby,' I said, 'she'd be less jealous of Lucasta.'

Ace filled up my glass.

'You get on all right with Lucasta, don't you?'

'Yes,' I said, 'but I'm not her step-mother. She's sweet, Lucasta, but she's learnt to be diplomatic. She can beam at Jack with one eye, and freeze Maggie with the other – all at the same time. And although I think Jack's lovely . . .'

'I gathered that, several times,' said Ace.

'Oh shut up,' I said. 'Not in that way. I know he's your brother and all that, but he's terribly insensitive towards Maggie. Always putting her down. I couldn't cope with it.'

'I hope to Christ they don't break up,' said Ace.

'To lose one wife looks like misfortune,' I said, 'but to lose two looks like carelessness. It's difficult to get anyone to take you seriously if you've got two marriages under your belt.'

'You're a perceptive child sometimes, aren't you?'

'Not about myself,' I said, gouging crosses in the brown sugar.

There was a pause.

Ace shot me a speculative glance. 'Pendle's the one who worries me really. He's heading for a crack-up if he's not careful.'

'Ah Pendle,' I said, tearing out the soft inside of my roll and kneading it into pellets. 'He only went after me because

I looked like Maggie, and he was trying to kick the habit.'

'You don't have to talk about it, if you don't want to.'

Suddenly I found I did.

'He took me back to his flat, and tried to pull me the first night we met. We'd been to a party. I was a bit tight, but when the crunch came he stopped in the middle. He simply couldn't bring himself to.'

I felt my face going very hot, and took another slug at my wine.

'It was awful, as though he really hated touching me, like a person making himself pick up toads. I think I knew it was no good for ages. But I've always been one to go on watering plants long after they're dead. I knew I was living in a fool's paradise.'

'Better than no paradise at all,' said Ace. 'He must have given you a hard time. I'm sorry.'

'Wasn't much fun, but in a way it was such a nightmare *during*, that afterwards hasn't been nearly so bad. Like the Red Queen pricking her finger – pain first, prick afterwards.'

'Pricks don't seem to have had much to do with it,' said Ace. 'I'm going to have a large brandy. Would you like one too?'

Later we wandered for miles along the shingle, the waves booming, the seagulls circling and complaining overhead. I suddenly looked at Ace – angular features softened, black hair slightly ruffled, suntan whipped up by the wind – and my stomach disappeared.

'You're very quiet,' he said. 'What are you thinking about?'

'Oh,' I stammered, 'I was just thinking how nice it is, and how I don't want to go back to work and my horrid old boss.'

'How old is he?'

'Quite old,' I said without thinking. 'He must be thirty,' and then realized what I'd said. 'I mean I only called him my old boss, like some people call their wives their old woman – when they're not old, I mean.'

'I see,' said Ace dryly.

When we got back to the car, we looked out to sea for a minute. Please God, make him kiss me, I prayed. I'll behave well for at least a year. God wasn't listening. Ace lit a cigarette.

'I came here with Elizabeth,' he said, 'not long before she died. It was a bitterly cold day. She used to feel the cold. I kept giving her pairs of gloves, but she always lost them. She had a whole drawer full of single gloves because she couldn't bear to throw away anything I'd given her.'

I found my eyes filling with tears.

'Does it still hurt – all the time?'

'It gets better – then one has terrible jabs like a war wound. It's pretty good hell being a "widower".' I could feel him carefully putting quotes around the word. 'Depression makes you lousy company. When you meet old mates you're reminded of previous times when you were together. You avoid happily married couples – you can't stand the togetherness. And you can feel yourself projecting your bitterness and indifference on to everyone else. However sympathetic people are, there's something humiliating about disaster. You always feel yourself being pitied or patronized.'

The dark eyes were brooding beneath the thick brows. What a splendidly strong face he had. He was not at all like the person I first thought – much more complicated and, though he didn't realize it, much more vulnerable.

'One feels guilty, too, about forgetting.'

'But you can't give up women for good,' I said.

'I don't – it's been two years now. Casual affairs are all right. But when you've had the sort of thing Elizabeth and I had casual affairs aren't really enough. On the other hand one feels guilty about becoming totally committed to someone else.'

He threw his cigarette out of the window and started up the car. It had suddenly got much, much colder. An apricot sun was firing the pine trees as we drove home. Some Pole was playing Chopin Nocturnes on the car wireless. Suddenly a black and white bird flashed across the road; it was a magpie. One for sorrow, two for joy. I looked frantically round for its mate. I'd had enough unhappiness recently, but there was no sight of another one.

'Not too tired?' he said.

'I feel marvellous.'

'We'll stop soon for a drink.'

An hour later I sat in a happy stupor, drinking a huge dry martini.

'Thank you for a heavenly day,' I said.

Ace smiled. 'It's not over yet. The food's good here. Would you like to stop for dinner?'

'Oh, yes please,' I said.

'I'll go and ring home.' I was expanding like a flower. But my daydreams were rudely interrupted.

'Afraid we've had dinner here,' he said. 'A couple of mates have turned up unexpectedly at home – arrived just after we left, and been cooling their heels waiting ever since – so we'd better go back. We can all eat out locally. I told Jack to book a table.'

We drove as fast as possible along the narrow roads, head-lamps lighting up stone walls hung with rusty bracken and fern. The wireless was playing Schubert's C Minor Symphony, and as various sections of the orchestra stalked catlike through the second movement, I tried to fight off bitter disappointment. No cosy tête-à-tête now, just Mulhollands scrapping all through dinner, with two more of Ace's friends clamouring for his attention, and no doubt having conversations about politics ten feet above my head. Ace suddenly seemed very uptight too. The lovely intimacy we'd built up during the day was disintegrating like an iced lolly at the end of its stick. It was all the fault of that bloody magpie.

'Look,' Ace said.

'Are they . . . ?' I began. We both started speaking at exactly the same time.

'No, you go on,' we both said.

There was a pause.

'Are they nice, your friends?' I said.

'You may know one of them – Jimmy Batten. He's a barrister; knows Pendle, I think.'

'Oh, I love him,' I said, perking up. 'He was prosecuting in Pendle's rape case. Who's the other bloke?'

'It's a girl,' said Ace. 'An American called Berenice de Courcy.'

'Sounds familiar,' I said. 'Doesn't she churn out best-sellers about raising one's consciousness? She's a big star in the States, isn't she?'

'That's right,' said Ace, slowing down to avoid a sheep.

'And ravishingly beautiful – "I can support the movement *and* shave my legs" sort of thing?'

'That's the one.'

'Trust Jimmy Batten to have someone like that in tow. I thought he was married.'

'Not very,' said Ace, putting his foot on the accelerator.

I wanted to put on some make-up to compete with the formidable Berenice, but there was not much I could do careering along in the dark. I nearly gouged out my eye with my mascara wand, then slapped on the dregs of a bottle of Diorissimo and had done with it.

CHAPTER TWELVE

THEY were all in the drawing-room when we got back. Neither Rose nor Maggie were looking their best. Rose had obviously had too much to drink and no time to wash her hair. A three-day-old fringe separated on her forehead, showing up lines, making her look much older than usual. Maggie was sulking and wearing too much make-up. Jimmy Batten stood with his back to the fire, nursing a large gin and tonic and exuding urbanity. He looked less attractive than I remembered him. His camel-coloured casual clothes were a little too tight, and clashed with his now drink-flushed face. His sleek, dapper otter good looks went much better with a dark suit. Jack, just back from the office, already with several large whiskies under his belt, was gazing at Berenice with undisguised admiration. And well he might, because she was *ravishing*, straight out of the pages of Harpers, with a mane of black hair rippling down her back, a long lean figure, slitty dark eyes, a wide red mouth and a conker brown suntan. She was wearing a black satin shirt, grey suède Gauchos clinched by a black Hermes belt, and black cowboy boots which showed off her terrific legs. And she exuded so much glossy good health she made everyone else look like hospital cases. Goodness, I thought, J. Batten has done well for himself. The next moment she had swiftly crossed the room to us.

'Ivan, sweetest,' she purred, taking both his hands, 'I know we should have warned you, but I got your letter, and you sounded so down I decided to come over myself instead of answering.'

Ace gave a slightly twisted smile, and kissed her smooth brown cheek.

'You were always one for surprises. I thought you were in Florida.'

'I got bored out of my mind with sunbathing. Then James 'phoned from New York, and persuaded me to come over.'

'Hullo Ace,' said Jimmy, grinning. 'I was guarding her from hi-jackers, honest I was.'

Then he gave me a great hug.

'Pru, my darling, I hear you've been terribly poorly. You do look a bit pulled down. Never mind, Berenice is the health freak round here. She'll soon pump you full of mega-vitamins and have you right as rain.'

'Hi, Prudence,' said Berenice, flashing her great white teeth at me. 'James hasn't stopped talking about you since we met.'

She turned back to Ace.

'How was Venezuela, darling? I read your piece on Sunday. It was terrific. Boy, can you empathize with the under-privileged! And I've got finished copies of *Brave Nutritional World*,' she went on, picking up a book with a large photograph of herself on the front. 'They're already re-printing. My British publishers really zapped out when they heard I was coming. The B.B.C. and Border have already been on, and I'm going to Granada in Manchester to-morrow.'

Ace laughed. 'You've certainly been busy.'

'Rose-Mary has been so gracious letting me use the 'phone,' said Berenice, smiling at Rose. 'You're quite right about your family, Ivan. I recognized Margaret and Rose-Mary, and of course Jack, immediately without being introduced. We've been verbalizing non-stop since we arrived.'

For a second I caught Jack's eye and started to giggle, then hastily turned it into a cough.

'I'll get you a drink,' said Jack, who wanted an excuse to re-fill his own. 'Sure you won't change your mind, Berenice? She refuses to drink anything but tomato juice,' he added to Ace.

Berenice smiled and said she didn't need alcohol, she was

'bombed out of her skull just meeting Ivan's folks'. She didn't seem quite so keen on the animals, giving Coleridge and Wordsworth vertical pats to keep them away whenever they approached her, and fussily brushing Antonia Fraser's ginger fur off the sofa – and her shirt.

'I don't mean to sound pressing,' said Jimmy Batten, as his glass was filled up, 'but I for one ought to mop up some alcohol soon.'

'I've booked a table at Dorothy's at 9.30,' said Jack.

Rose peered at her face in her powder compact, then calmly got a pair of pants out of her bag and cleaned the glass with them. Berenice determinedly didn't look shocked.

'You can count me out,' said Rose, putting pants and mirror away and getting to her feet. 'I'm going to wash my hair and go to bed early.'

'I'm going to change,' I said.

'Are they staying the night?' I said to Rose as we went upstairs.

'Yes. Mrs. Braddock's made up a bed.'

'Hadn't they better have my room,' I said, 'It's got a double bed.'

'Oh no sweetie, it's not worth shifting your things just for one night. Jimmy's going early tomorrow morning. He can have Linn's room, and Berenice'll be sleeping with Ace.'

I clutched the banisters for support.

'I thought she was Jimmy's girlfriend,' I whispered.

'Oh no, darling. She and Ace have been living together in New York for the past six months.'

'Are you sure?' I said.

'Of course I am,' said Rose rather acidly. 'She's spent all afternoon, when she wasn't on the telephone, telling us what a "warm beautiful human being" Ace is. I hope she's tough enough to cope with him.'

Once in my room, despair overwhelmed me. To be *so* unprepared. To have no idea I had fallen so totally in love, only to find it was hopeless. And to think I'd been presumptuous enough to imagine that a man in Ace's class could possibly fancy someone as young and unsophisticated as me. It was ludicrous.

I didn't cry. It's funny, you don't when something really cataclysmic happens. I sat on the bed trembling and dry eyed, clutching the kitten who purred noisily, and grooved the side of its face against my chin.

Desperately I cast around for some kind of comfort, but there was none. No lifebelts, no driftwood, no passing ships.

'Oh no,' I whispered. 'No, no, no.'

There was a knock on the door. My heart leapt. Perhaps it was Ace come to say it was all some horrible mistake. But it was Lucasta in tears.

'I can't find my foxy,' she sobbed. 'I've looked for him everywhere.'

'He's in the hot cupboard,' I said. 'We put him there after he fell in the bath yesterday.'

'Oh, so we did. Please don't go away again. I've been left with Mrs. Braddock all day. I wasn't allowed in the drawing-room because Bare Knees is there. She said she just loved children; then she kept telling me to go away. Granny says she's going to marry Ace. I hope she doesn't. At twelve o'clock tonight, I can say tomorrow's my birthday. You will stay for my party, won't you?'

Would I? I was tempted to bolt straight back to London, but couldn't bear to tear myself away quite yet.

'Oh look,' said Lucasta, running to the window.

Snow was beginning to fall. A glistening, crumbling drift had formed on the window ledge. Now a storm of big flakes swept giddily by.

'Tomorrow we can make a snowman. Oh, I wish I had a sledge.'

I looked at myself in the mirror. My reflection stared back pale and hollow-eyed, with the exhausted gritted-teeth look of a candidate who's just lost his seat. What the hell could I wear tonight? Ace had seen everything I'd brought. All my seductive clothes were in London, anyway, except for my green culotte dress, which was much too naked, and went too well with my little green face.

In the end I kept my jeans on, and put on a white slightly see-through shirt. Not that there's much to see any more, I thought gloomily. Then I discovered I'd left my only decent eye-shadow behind in the pub at lunchtime. It seemed centuries ago, when I was happy.

Ace was waiting in the hall.

He'd changed into a suit and a pink shirt. Oh the beauty of those broad pinstriped shoulders, and long, long legs. I could smell his aftershave. I felt faint with longing.

'Are you sure you're up to going out?' he said.

I could read the compassion in his eyes.

'I'm fine,' I snapped, absolutely terrified of betraying myself.

Dorothy's restaurant was named after Dorothy Words-worth. It had soft lighting, black beams, framed photostats of pages from Dorothy Wordsworth's diary on the white-washed walls, and forced daffodils on every table. It was pretty but a bit twee. Berenice, however, absolutely freaked out, standing in the doorway of the dining-room in her huge wolf coat, shrieking,

'My God, I am not ready for this! I am simply not ready for this!'

'Well if you're not, I am,' said Jimmy Batten briskly. 'Come on, Pru. You go in first. I'll sit next to you.'

Maggie sat on the other side, with Jack opposite me, and Berenice next to him, and then Ace. So at least I didn't have to spend all dinner directly avoiding his eyes. Berenice made a great deal of palaver about removing her coat and entrusting it to the waiter, until everyone in the restaurant was staring at us.

'Isn't this place just darling?' she went on, glancing round at the couples in the alcoves. 'We *must* come here on our own one evening, Ivan darling.'

She was slightly less amused when she consulted the menu, which took up the whole table, and discovered there were no vegetarian dishes.

'I forgot you were all on this carnivore trip over here,' she said. 'Can you have a word with the waiter, Ivan? They might have some egg plant lasagne or some lentils.'

'They're not into all that macrobiotic crap over here,' said Ace. 'This is England.'

'Oh well,' said Berenice, looking martyred, 'I'll just settle for veggies and sour cream this evening.'

'I'd like an enormous steak, very rare, and chips,' Jack said to the waiter. 'And tell the wine waiter to step on it.'

'We're not into gourmet tripping any more in the States,' said Berenice. 'I just ask people to drop around and take pot luck.'

'And then dump another quart of water in the lentil soup,' said Jimmy Batten, spreading butter thickly on a roll.

Berenice looked at him in disapproval. 'You don't realize what white flour does to you, James. It amazes me the garbage you British eat. Ivan was living on hamburgers when I met him. No wonder he nearly had an ulcer.'

'When's your new book coming out?' said Jack.

'In January. It's being translated into fifteen languages.'

'It ought to be translated into English first,' said Ace.

'Oh starp, sweetest, starp,' said Berenice, laughing. 'He's so vile about my literary style. Being an academic, I'm afraid I'm used to writing for an optimum intellectual readership. You know I can't believe I'm in Ivan's home town at last.'

'We can't quite believe you're here either,' said Jack. 'We're going to need at least four bottles, Ace.'

'Such a relief going into a restaurant where I'm not known,' said Berenice. 'In the States I can't cross the street without being mobbed.'

She's utterly poisonous, I thought.

'Cheer up, darling,' whispered Jimmy Batten in my ear. 'How's Pendle?'

'He's coming up on Saturday to collect me,' I said.

'Not going very well?'

I shook my head.

'Thought as much.' He lowered his voice. 'Still after Maggie? Poor old you. I should have warned you when we met in London. Maggie looks terrible too. I've never seen such a deterioration in anyone. She used to be *so* pretty.'

The dinner seemed to go on for ever. I had to force myself to get any food down, taking frequent gulps of wine. Ace was talking to Jimmy Batten about delinquency in New York. Berenice was going on and on about Jack's unimaginative life style. 'You ought to cut out that nine to five shit,' she said, waving a cauliflower floweret in the air, 'and get in touch with the universe.'

'I can't really cut it out,' protested Jack. 'I've got two households to support.'

Now Berenice was rabbiting on about her last husband. 'I wanted an open living relationship based on trust and growth, and all he wanted was his jockey shorts ironed. I mean we weren't coming from the same place *at* all.'

'And Ace doesn't expect you to do his ironing?' said Jack. Suddenly I felt his ankle rubbing up and down against mine.

'Oh, starp. Don't make comparisons,' said Berenice, putting one of her lovely sunburned hands on Jack's arm. 'Ivan is just terrific. He gives off this incredible togetherness, it's beautiful. We have these terrifically productive dialogues, sitting around for hours rapping.'

'Surprised you don't find him too forceful,' said Jack.

'Well he's a Leo of course,' admitted Berenice. 'They're very big on macho tripping, but he's trying to overcome it.'

For a second I met Ace's eye, found myself blushing and looked away.

'I was a big star, of course, when I met Ivan,' Berenice went on. 'But my life was empty. I needed a whole, loving, caring environment, where I could be totally committed. You've no idea the creases he's taken out of my mind.'

'So Ace is the one who's doing the ironing,' said Jack, gravely.

Berenice didn't flicker. She was not to be deflected. She was in such full flood she didn't even notice when Jack rolled a tonic bottle across the table towards me. Inside on a bit of paper he'd written 'Help'.

I took it out, and wrote 'I love you' on the back, and rolled it back again. It was a comfort that he thought her as silly as I did. But she was certainly mad for Ace. She'd reached the stage now when she couldn't bear not to touch him. Her free hand strayed now to his hair, now to the nape of his neck, now to his thigh.

Then she decided I needed bringing in and asked me what I thought of Northern Ireland, but my mouth was still full of dry, unswallowable chicken, so I just shook my head, and she said she thought people's capacity for outrage in this country was amazingly dulled.

Then it was Maggie's turn. She was wearing the shirt Ace had brought her from the States.

'I'm so glad you're wearing that shirt, Margaret. Ivan and I must have gone to a dozen shops to find the right colour.' Then she turned to Ace, licking him on the ear. 'And you've no idea the free gift I've got for you later darling,' she said huskily.

I couldn't bear any more. I could feel the sweat rising on my forehead, it was so hot.

'Must go to the loo,' I muttered, wriggling round the table, and scuttling across the restaurant.

When I came out I found Jimmy Batten.

'I'll take you home,' he said.

'Oh, please.' I felt sick and giddy, very near to tears.

'I'll just go and tell everyone.'

'Could you just get a waiter to tell them after we've gone?' I couldn't face Ace at the moment.

The snow was thickening as we drove home, settling in the arms of trees and on the tops of walls and gates. As we reached the end of the village, and started on the road up to the Mulhollands' house we passed a large notice, saying: 'Unfenced Road, beware of animals.'

'It's not the animals you have to beware of round here,' I said bitterly.

'It's not Pendle any more, is it?' said Jimmy Batten.

'Oh God, is it that obvious?'

'Only to me. I could never understand what a larky girl

like you could see in Pendle. He's like a synopsis. Ace is a whole book.'

'Is it a very big thing, him and Berenice?'

' 'Tis for her. She talks a lot of crap about L.T.R. – Living Together Relationships as she calls them – but she'd do anything to get him up the aisle. I guess he's the one who's putting up the sandbags. He's not ready to marry anyone yet.'

'What's so marvellous about her?' I said dismally.

'Superior muscle tone, darling. She's a very ballsy lady. She's terrific in the sack. She used to be a girlfriend of mine. I couldn't cope with the neurotics, but maybe Ace can handle her.'

'I see,' I said listlessly.

'Poor little Pru.' Jimmy put out a hand and touched my cheek. 'You haven't had much luck with the Mulhollands, have you?'

After he'd seen me upstairs he said, 'I'm leaving at crack of dawn tomorrow. I've got a case in Birmingham. Ring me when you get back to London. I'll buy you dinner.'

I got into bed and read the same page over and over again. Then I got Pendle's photograph out of my top drawer. It was tattered and creased from being hawked around in my bag for so long. It was as though I was looking at a total stranger. How could I have ever loved him? Beside Ace he seemed a complete shadow.

It was after midnight when I heard them coming home. The snow was six inches deep on the windowsill. There was a knock on my door. It was Ace. He came and sat down on the bed.

'Why didn't you tell me you felt bad? I'd have brought you home.'

'You were otherwise engaged,' I said bleakly.

He looked at me in silence, the tassels of the bedside lamp fretting a shadow across his left cheekbone.

'You looked miserable all evening. I was watching you.'

'I hope you learnt something,' I snapped, shifting my legs irritably. Next moment Pendle's photograph had fluttered down on to the floor. Ace picked it up and looked at it for a minute.

'I see. Have you been talking to Jimmy?'

'Yes,' I said tonelessly. What did a thumping lie matter now? 'Seeing him brought the whole Pendle thing back.'

'You've had a long day. One doesn't get over these things all at once, and they always seem worse when you're tired.'

I felt my chin trembling. It was the onset of tears again. Ace put his hand out, but I flinched away. If he touched me, I knew I was lost.

'Don't. I can't bear it.'

He sighed, took my book from me and switched off the bedroom lamp. 'Try and get some sleep.'

I heard his bedroom door open and shut. My body seemed to burn as I tossed and turned. I must forget about him. I must stop imagining all the things he and Berenice would be doing in a minute. I wondered if he'd removed Elizabeth's picture before he got to work. Large tears rolled out of the corners of my eyes. The night seemed to go on and on. One thing could be said in favour of falling in love with Ace, it was going to make dying a whole lot of fun.

CHAPTER THIRTEEN

WHEN I woke next morning, I could see dirty flakes of snow falling outside the window. I had only half-drawn the curtains. The snow was coming down sideways now, slanting to the left. If I stared at it long enough, I felt giddy. I closed my eyes, but knew I wouldn't get back to sleep again. Gradually I pieced together yesterday's events and groaned. Really they ought to found a Pre-Marriage Guidance Council for people like me. Pendle was due in two days. Perhaps if it kept on snowing the roads would get blocked up and he'd never arrive.

There was a knock on the door and Mrs. Braddock came in with a red nose and a breakfast tray, followed by Coleridge, the kitten swinging on his back legs.

'Lovely weather,' said Mrs. Braddock. 'The snow came over my ankles when I opened the back door. Someone will have to shovel it away, but it won't be me.'

'You shouldn't have bothered,' I said, wriggling into a sitting position. 'I was going to come down.'

'Mr. Ace insisted. He said you're to eat it all, as you didn't touch your dinner last night, and to remember your medicine.'

'You are kind,' I said, valiantly trying to work up some enthusiasm for bacon and eggs. 'Is he having breakfast?'

'Gone down to mill with Mr. Jack. Mr. Batten's left. He's a *nice* gentleman, and *she's* up already, poking around the kitchen, giving orders, asking questions.'

'Who?' I said.

Mrs. Braddock was suddenly a picture of outraged dignity.

'Berenice or whatever she calls herself. Waited until Mr. Ace had gone, then down she came poking into my larder, saying we were all poisoning ourselves with chemicals, and threw all my packets of cake mix in the dustbin. I've cooked for this family for thirty years, hardly a day of sickness. Never known such a healthy lot.'

'Nor have I. They must have constitutions like oxen to survive all that booze.'

'She's even given me a shopping list,' puffed Mrs. Braddock. 'Where can I find soya beans and brown rice and courgettes and bran in the village in the middle of winter?'

I giggled. 'Get Mr. Braddock to make her up a bran mash down at the stables.'

'Well I must get back to my kitchen. The washing machine's acting very strange and Miss Maggie left the Professor's hat in the hall and Antonia Fraser slept on it last night and squashed it flat as a pancake.'

'The cat sat on the 'at,' I said, feeling slightly better. I got up, gave the bacon and eggs to Coleridge, who already had long trails of saliva hanging from either side of his mouth, and waved at Lucasta who was building a snowman in the garden.

In the drawing-room I found Berenice looking like something out of *Country Life*, wearing an olive green cashmere twinset, a brown tweed skirt, beautiful casual shoes with stacked heels, and listening to Vivaldi. She was obviously being thwarted in her attempts to spend a morning *en famille*.

'Doesn't anyone ever get up here? That poor old woman who's quite past it is having to do everything. I've never seen anything like the dirt in this house, dog hair everywhere, and I've just spent half an hour cleaning the john.'

'The what? Oh, the loo,' I said.

She took a bottle of brown tablets out of her bag. 'Here are the multi-vitamin tablets I promised you. I'd take four if I were you, three times a day.'

'Gosh thanks,' I said, feeling perhaps I'd misjudged her.

'Are you into Yoga, Prudence?' she said, flexing her neck gracefully. 'Whenever I get tense, I sit down and meditate.

I've got a book on the subject. I'll lend it to you. I'm sure it would help you get it together with Pendle.'

Interfering old busybody. I wondered how much Ace had told her.

Now she was walking around the room examining everything.

'This room could be so charming if only someone bothered. In my apartment in New York I've gone back to natural fibres and earthy colours. I mean, environment is terrifically important to one's inner serenity.'

She'd have that red wallpaper out in a flash. I wondered, if I really tried, if I could ever be as beautiful as she was and decided not. Standing by the window, with her glowing suntan, and the snowy mountains behind, she was rather like a winter sports poster. Perhaps Mrs. Braddock would come in yodelling and bearing Gluwein.

'What does Rose-Mary do all day, apart from squandering Ivan's inheritance?' asked Berenice.

'Well, it's a good question. She's got lots of friends, plays bridge, looks beautiful, and – er – has fun.'

'And Margaret? She's really out of shape; her derrière follows her upstairs.'

'Well, the same really,' I said lamely, 'but she seems to have less fun.'

'I got very negative vibes from her last night. I guess she and Jack aren't getting it together. I must have a good rap with her later, about redefining the parameters of their relationship.'

She got up and turned Vivaldi over to the flip side.

'This is the only record that hasn't got scratches.'

'I don't expect anyone's ever played it,' I said. 'I suppose we'd better start thinking about Lucasta's party.'

'I'm an expert on kids' parties,' said Berenice smugly. 'Last summer I gave an all night party for my son Che. He's the same age as Lucasta, but super intelligent.'

'How on earth did you keep them all amused all that time?'

'Oh we didn't bother with games. I provided a running

buffet, soya bean canapes, carrot cake and my lentil loaf, and the kids wrote their own scenario as the party went along.'

At that moment Lucasta barged in, emitting Tarzan howls and leaving the door open.

'Will you come and see my snowman?' she said, kneeling down by the fire and holding her hands to the flames. 'D'you think the lake's going to freeze over? Can I have a biscuit?'

'*May* I have a biscuit,' corrected Berenice with a charming smile. 'A raw carrot would be much better for you.'

'I'm not a donkey. Are you coming, Pru?'

'Is your Mummy up yet?' said Berenice, ignoring her rudeness.

'She's not my Mummy,' hissed Lucasta. 'She's my father's wife.'

Almost on cue Maggie came through the door. She shot a venomous look at Lucasta but didn't say anything. She looked very pale.

'Are you all right?' I said.

'So, so. Look, Jack's on the telephone; you wouldn't like to have a word with him?'

I went into the hall and picked up the receiver.

'Baby!' said Jack. 'Are you better? How's the Great American disaster?'

'Heavy.'

He laughed. 'You wouldn't like to have lunch with me? Then afterwards we can choose Lucasta's presents, and get the things for the party.'

'Oh, I'd love to. What about Maggie? She looks rotten,' I said. 'Doesn't she want to come with us?'

'Not in the least. I'll pick you up about one o'clock.'

Back in the drawing-room Berenice was starting her Ancient Mariner act on Maggie.

'I exercise every morning,' she was saying. 'Exercises aimed at the stomach, the tarps of the legs and whole pelvic area that one uses for sex. Start using those internal muscles and everything improves, and I mean everything, Margaret.'

She smiled warmly at Maggie. 'I'm sure you and Jack can work it through.'

Ace came back at lunchtime with Jack, who said he'd just flip through his mail and we'd be off. Maggie was still in her dressing-gown. Rose hadn't surfaced. Berenice was flapping around about going on television in Manchester that evening.

'The producer has said don't bother to dress up.'

Would her French jeans and Hermes belt be too casual? What time did Ace think they ought to start? Would the roads be bad? I saw Ace stifle a yawn. He looked absolutely knackered. Too much of Berenice's superior muscle tone, I thought sourly. Having been so crochety with him last night, I found it very difficult to act normally now. We were acidly polite to each other. I still couldn't look him straight in the eye.

The telephone rang. Maggie shot out of the room to answer it. Normally Jack wouldn't be home at this time of day. I wondered idly if it was Pendle ringing.

Berenice turned to Ace. 'Shall I make an egg plant lasagne for this evening, sweetest? We could heat it up when we get back.'

Ace said that he'd much rather eat out.

Maggie poked her head round the door. 'It's for you, Ace,' she said. 'It's Penelope Blake.'

'You look a bit uptight, sweetest,' said Berenice, when Ace came back five minutes later. 'Shall I massage your neck?'

'I am *not* uptight,' snapped Ace. 'That was Elizabeth's mother confirming lunch tomorrow. I'm sorry,' he added to Jack, 'it was arranged before I knew about Lucasta's party. I can't really stand them up.'

'Course you can't,' said Jack, throwing a pile of envelopes into the wastepaper basket.

'You'll miss my party,' wailed Lucasta.

Ace pulled her on to his knee. 'No I won't lovie. It's only forty miles away. I should get back by five if the snow doesn't get any worse.'

'I'm so much looking forward to meeting Elizabeth's folks tomorrow,' said Berenice. 'I'm sure we can be very supportive.'

'I'm afraid I've got to go on my own,' said Ace bluntly. 'I haven't seen them since the funeral. It wouldn't be very tactful to barge in with someone else.'

Berenice shook back her dark hair angrily. Suddenly there was a muscle going in her cheek.

'And what am I supposed to do while you're away?'

'You can help Pru organize the party.'

Lunch with Jack was a blissful relief. We both drank too much and I told Jack about Berenice's plans for re-vamping the drawing-room.

'She'll have my mother jogging in a track suit and Mrs. Braddock in an old people's home by Christmas. We'll all be out at the rate she's going.'

'She believes in clearing the decks,' I said gloomily, 'and she isn't too choosy who she sweeps into the sea.'

'She's certainly put the kibosh on Ace. He could hardly walk this morning. Never actually came near the mill at all. Just sloped off to see an osteopath about his bad back.'

I giggled. Jack always had the ability to make things seem less awful.

'I expect you'll be round at the osteopath tomorrow,' I said. 'Berenice has been giving Maggie a few tips on sexual technique.'

Jack took my hand, 'When you said "I love you" in that tonic bottle last night, did you mean it?'

'Yes,' I said, 'brother-sister.'

'We'll always be friends, won't we? Christ, how maudlin can one get? What the hell am I going to do about Maggie?'

'You could boost her morale a bit more,' I said.

Afterwards, expansive from drink, we went shopping, buying party food and three cases of Entre deux Mers – to cheer up the mothers, said Jack. Then we spent a fortune at the toyshop, buying loads of little presents for the party and a red and silver sleigh and a three-foot fluffy white rabbit as main presents for Lucasta. I bought her a black velvet cat suit I thought she might like to wear to the party.

'It's so much easier shopping with you than Maggie,' sighed Jack. 'She always gets green eyes when I spend money on Lucasta.'

When we got back, Ace and Berenice had gone. I found Maggie eating chocolate cake in the kitchen.

'What are you doing in here?' I said.

'It's the warmest room. The central heating's given up the ghost. Berenice and I have been having a terrifically productive dialogue. Jack and I have got to work through our conflicts and stop laying bad trips on each other, and re-structure our marriage.'

'That's nice,' said Jack, coming in with a tumbler half full of whisky and heading for the fridge. 'You can start off by putting a couple of my shirts in the washing machine.'

'That's broken too,' said Maggie. 'It went bananas this afternoon. It was like Lake Windermere in here an hour ago.'

'Well you can wash a shirt by hand,' said Jack. 'Tomorrow is my daughter's birthday. I have important customers coming over. I need a clean shirt. Christ, isn't anyone ever going to de-frost this fridge?'

'I am *not* going to wash your shirt, Jack,' said Maggie, her voice rising, 'just because I am a female person. You are a microcosm of the whole male power base. Don't you know the whole macho number is sick?'

'Oh boy,' said Jack, 'that is profound. I think you've been talking to Berenice. I can't even get the ice tray out, but I would have thought you and Ms. de Courcy would have provided enough hot air to melt it.'

'Can't we even have a meaningful dialogue? You've been on a macho trip all your life, Jack.'

'Oh, shut up.'

'I'm entitled to my own opinions.'

'Of course you are. I don't want to hear them, that's all.'

'Oh, I hate you,' sobbed Maggie, rushing out of the room and slamming the door behind her.

'At least that might loosen the ice tray,' said Jack.

Later we watched Berenice on television. She was wearing a man's grey flannel suit, a white shirt and the inevitable Hermes belt.

'She's certainly easy on the eye,' I said.

'And absolute hell on the ears,' said Jack.

I was safely in bed by the time they came home – but this time Ace didn't bother to come and say good night.

CHAPTER FOURTEEN

THE good thing about Lucasta's birthday party was that I was so busy I didn't have much time to brood. After a lousy night, I got up early. It was bitterly cold, the central heating was still kaput, and there were frost patterns like doilies all over the windows. I put on a thick grey sweater over two other sweaters, rust shorts, tights, leg warmers, and boots, and I was still cold. I went down to the kitchen to help Mrs. Braddock make sausage rolls and fillings for the sandwiches. She was still muttering about Berenice. I was mindlessly mixing salad cream with hard-boiled eggs when Jack came in on his way to the office.

'Knock, knock,' he said.

'Who's there?'

'Ivan.'

'Ivan who?'

'Ivan 'orrible 'eadache. I haven't actually, its Maggie. She's complaining of a migraine; may be diplomatic because of Lucasta's party – but she looks pretty rough, probably suffering from an overdose of Berenice yesterday. I'm sorry to dump all this on you. There's still the bridge rolls, the cake, some meringues and eclairs to be collected from the village, and the conjuror'll be here by 4.45.'

He picked up his brief case. 'I'll come home soon as I'm shot of these Americans. Will you be all right?'

'I'd rather cope with thirty children than Berenice,' I said.

'Send them all out for a run in the snow,' said Jack. 'And offer £500 as a prize to the one who comes home last.'

A blackbird suddenly tapped its yellow beak on the frosted window, peering in at us with inquisitive bright eyes.

'I'd stay outside if I were you,' I said. 'It's much warmer out there.'

Ace came down looking even more heavy-eyed than yesterday, presumably from another night of passion.

'How's your bad back?' I said sweetly.

He shot me a dirty look and went off and vented his rage on the gas board. 'There are women and children freezing to death over here,' I could hear him saying. 'For Christ sake, can't you put chains on your vans? I want someone over here immediately.'

Lucasta was delighted with her presents. Ace had given her Snoopy in a Snoopy kennel handbag from the States. Berenice gave her a flower press and spent a lot of time explaining that Lucasta mustn't use it on Granny's cyclamens but must wait until the summer.

'Granny gave me a give-outcher from Harrods,' Lucasta told me, 'but I like the sledge, and Snoopy and your velvet cat suit best.'

I went upstairs to see Maggie. She was huddled in bed, a brimming ashtray beside her, looking terrible.

'I'll try and get up later,' she said. 'Did you know today was the first day of the rest of your life?'

'Another of Berenice's profundities,' I said crossly.

'I think it's rather good.'

'It's been said before.'

'Berenice doesn't seem very keen on you,' said Maggie.

'Oh,' I said, 'What did she say about me?'

'It was yesterday. I was saying you were pretty. She said your looks were rather *ordinaire,* and she didn't consider you a woman of substance.'

'Bloody bitch,' I said crossly. 'What else did she say?'

But Maggie was gazing out at the white landscape. 'Today is the first day of the rest of my life,' she said dreamily. 'I'm going to take a lover, the question is whose.'

I'd just finished making jellies and filling the meringues

with cream, and was making a hideous hedgehog by sticking cubes of pineapple and cheese on sticks into a grapefruit half, when Berenice arrived down, looking radiantly businesslike in black wool trousers, a red shirt and her hair tied back in a red bandana.

'Aren't you frozen?' I said.

'Of course not,' she said briskly. 'My exercises whip up the circulation. Where's Ivan?' she went on, pouring out her revolting health food breakfast that looked like rat droppings in sawdust.

'Trying out the new sledge with Lucasta.'

'And Rose-Mary and Margaret?'

'Still in bed,' I said, chopping up some more pieces of cheese, and giving a bit to the dogs who were slobbering at my feet.

Berenice looked annoyed. 'They're not being very supportive are they? After all, Lucasta *is* Jack's biological daughter.'

Brushing some non-existent hairs off her trousers, she stepped over Coleridge to get some milk from the fridge.

'Those damn dogs are moulting everywhere, and I'm sure I found a flea in our bed this morning.'

'It's much too cold for fleas,' said Ace coming in at the back door with Lucasta. There were snow flakes on his hair and his moustache. He looked cold and cross like Simpkin in *The Tailor of Gloucester*.

Back home after picking everything up from the village, Mrs. Braddock and I were spreading chopped eggs on bridge rolls, trying not to listen to Berenice giving a blow by blow account of how she made soya bean canapes. Ace was blowing up balloons. They were playing carols on the wireless. God, I thought dismally, it'll be Christmas in a couple of weeks. How the hell was I going to survive all the festivities? My thoughts careered wildly towards Ace, kissing me under the mistletoe, handing me a present in front of the tree, and careered away again. No doubt he'd spend Christmas enjoying Berenice in some four-star Paris hotel.

Lucasta sat on the table, eating Maltesers and swinging her legs, and telling us the plot of her nativity play.

'Then the angel Gabriel appears to Mary and announces her, and then he goes to the shepherds and says Piece of Earth, good will to all men.'

I caught Ace's eye and giggled.

It was midday. Everyone except Berenice had been banished from the kitchen, so she could give her all to her carrot cake. Even Ace had been thrown out. She was sulking because he refused to try one of her soya bean canapes. The dogs were behaving appallingly, because no one had had time to take them for a proper walk. Mrs. Braddock was trying to clean the hall floor, putting down newspapers to dry it as she went. Wordsworth sat just behind her whining querulously. Coleridge had just eaten a whole plate of sausages, and then rushed off upstairs. I found him rolling around on Ace and Berenice's bed, wiping his face on their counterpane. Elizabeth's photograph had been removed from the bedside, I noticed. Fifteen love to Berenice.

I went downstairs and gathered up the balloons, climbing on to the hall table to pin them in a bunch from the ceiling. Suddenly, I was overcome by dizziness, and felt myself swaying.

The next moment two hands grabbed me firmly round the hips and steadied me.

I looked down and blushed scarlet. It was Ace. He was wearing a navy blue overcoat with the velvet collar turned up, obviously just going out. My fingers were suddenly all thumbs. I took ages to tie the string. When I finished he lifted me down, and just for a second held me, frowning down at me.

'Let me go,' I muttered, terrified once more that I was going to cry.

'Stop fighting,' he said softly. 'I've got enough people bitching at me today without you joining them.'

I tried to smile. 'I'm sorry.'

He let go of me. 'Now for Christ's sake remember how ill

you've been, and don't overdo it. Lie down for a couple of hours after lunch. The man'll be over to do the central heating any minute.'

He went towards the door.

'I hope it isn't too agonizing going to see them,' I stammered. 'I'm sure it'll mean a lot to them. You will drive carefully, won't you?'

'Of course.' He opened the door, letting in a blast of icy air.

'By the way, I like your leg warmers,' he said.

'They're my supportive hose,' I said.

Just for a second a smile flickered across his face.

Back in the kitchen Berenice was pounding lentils with unnecessary violence, her mouth set in a hard line.

'I am trying to remain supportive at the moment, but Ivan is being very difficult,' she said. 'Instead of being on the same wavelength, he's giving off a lot of static. He was so different in the States. It's the effect of his family of course. They're absolutely hopeless.'

'But he adores them.'

'They wear him down. And why does he have this morbid obsession with the past? It's so hypocritical. Elizabeth's parents have got to face up to the fact that he's bound to make another commitment sooner or later.'

'But they're old,' I said, removing Antonia Fraser who was thoughtfully licking crab paste off the bridge rolls, 'and they all loved Elizabeth.'

Crash came the pestle down on the poor lentils.

'That marriage'd have come unstuck anyway.'

'Rubbish,' I said furiously. 'He adored her. Everyone says so.'

'He'd never have achieved his full potential married to her. He'd have got bored.'

'Because she wasn't a woman of substance,' I said sourly. 'I suppose you would have found her a little *ordinaire*.'

Berenice's face suddenly took on the unarresting personality of a stopped clock. 'God rest you merry gentlemen,' sang the wireless.

163

I escaped from the kitchen before I wrung her deeply tanned neck.

Lucasta met me in the hall. 'Very bad news,' she said. 'Coleridge has been sick three times on the stairs, and there's bits of leather in it.'

'Oh God!'

From a cursory examination of the stairs it was quite obvious that Coleridge had regurgitated a good deal of chewed-up Hermes belt.

'Shall I tell Berenice?' asked Lucasta happily.

'God no,' I said. 'Do you want Coleridge put in an Old Setters' Home?'

'Don't look so sad,' said Lucasta to me as I mopped away with a Jay cloth and disinfectant. She put her arm round my shoulders.

'You may not be very clever,' she said, 'but you're very good at wiping up sick.'

At that moment Rose came down the stairs, carrying a suitcase. She looked very crestfallen. In fact her crest was positively round her ankles.

'Beastly, beastly weather,' she said.

'You're not going away, Granny?' said Lucasta.

'No darling, I'm going to have lunch and a nice hot bath at Professor Copeland's and change into something pretty for your party. Where is she?' she whispered, looking round nervously.

'Making health food canapes in the kitchen.'

Rose shuddered. 'She keeps trying to interest me in Yoga.'

'She thinks her navel is the centre of the universe.'

'I used to think naval officers were the centre of mine,' said Rose sadly.

There still seemed to be an awful lot to do. Hiding the going-away presents in a special drawer, putting cream in the meringues, hanging doughnuts on pieces of string, on a clothes line across the drawing-room. The child that finished its doughnut first, eating with its hands behind its back, would be awarded a prize. It was an excellent ice-breaker, said Berenice. I drew a donkey for people to pin a tail on. Berenice did an incredibly neat parcel for Pass-the-Parcel, using string instead of Sellotape. The snow was getting thicker, blanketing everything. I hoped Ace was getting on all right. Finally the man came to mend the central heating.

Maggie came down an hour before the party was due to start, poured herself a large drink, and balefully surveyed the platefuls of food in the kitchen.

'It looks like the planet of the Canapes,' she said.

Berenice's lips tightened at such 'unsupportive' behaviour, but she merely extracted the Vim from the cupboard under the sink and went towards the door.

'Where are you going?' said Lucasta.

'To have a bath,' said Berenice grimly.

'Gosh, you *must* be dirty!'

'This is to clean the bath before I get into it.'

CHAPTER FIFTEEN

I HAD hoped to have a bath too and change, but Berenice pinched all the hot water, and at the end there was a terrible rush, what with trying to find some candle holders for Lucasta's cake and getting her dressed and doing her hair. The Sting was pounding away in an empty drawing-room. I had only one eye made up when the doorbell rang. It was a mother, twenty minutes early.

'Awfully sorry,' she said. 'I didn't know how much time to leave because of the snow.'

And in no time the hall seemed to be full of Sophies, Pollys, Emilies and Katies, milling round in their long party dresses like coloured butterflies, watching Lucasta – the most ravishing of all in her black velvet cat suit – tearing open her presents. I was charging round like a scalded cat telling mothers where to put their coats, trying to open bottles of Entre deux Mers, answering the door and keeping the dogs off the food. Where the hell was everyone?

Then there was that terrible lull when half the children had arrived and you didn't know whether to start a game or not. None of the children were Lucasta's special friends, because the party wasn't being given at her own home, but just offspring of various local friends of the Mulhollands, so they were all very shy to begin with and stood around gazing at each other.

Very done up mothers and nannies wandered round looking disappointed and saying, 'We expected Ace, or at least Jack to be here.'

'They're coming later,' I said.

I charged upstairs. I found Maggie on the telephone in Rose's room. 'All right my sweetheart,' she was saying huskily, 'I'll call you later.' She blushed absolutely scarlet when she saw me standing in the doorway, and slammed down the receiver.

'Please come down and help,' I wailed. 'I can't do everything.'

'What do you want me to do?' she said, following me downstairs.

'Just shepherd them into the drawing-room, and start the children on the doughnut-eating race. The winner gets a wrapped-up prize. They're in the drawer of the sideboard. Oh God, there's the doorbell.'

It was a glamorous but rather grubby brunette in a sheepskin coat.

'Hi. I'm Delphinium,' she said vaguely. 'I brought Damian and Midas,' pointing to two very beautiful long-haired boys, one blond, one dark, who nearly knocked me sideways as they charged past me into the drawing-room.

'I left Lucasta's present behind,' she said, drifting after them. 'Can I help myself to a drink? I know where it's kept.'

The Muppet Show record had succeeded The Sting on the gramophone as Maggie came back into the hall.

'Hi, Delphinium,' she said, then turning to me, 'I'm afraid Coleridge and Wordsworth have got into the drawing-room and eaten half the doughnuts. They've gone really wild today.'

It was all too much. I started to giggle helplessly.

'It's because they can't verbalize their feelings,' I said. 'I guess they're getting negative vibes from a certain person, and they're just overreacting. Oh well, we'd better play Pass-the-Parcel.'

That wasn't much of a success either, because Berenice had done up the knots so beautifully no one could undo them. So we played musical bumps. But so many children had perfected the lightning descent, they kept dead-heating, and the ones already out, who included Damian and Midas, got bored and started a punch-up.

A diversion was created by the doorbell, and the arrival of

Jason, a sickly looking child in a green velvet suit, who turned out to be the sworn enemy of Damian and Midas.

'Oh bugger,' said Lucasta, tearing open Jason's present, 'another boring flower press.'

At that moment, Berenice chose to make her entrance, wearing a rust shirt, tan boots, and a black skirt with a slit up the front. Her newly washed hair gleamed – no wonder there wasn't any hot water left for me. She looked a million dollars and extremely irritated.

'You haven't seen my Hermes belt have you, Prudence?'

'Who wants to stick the tail on the donkey?' I shouted.

The fun became more fast and furious. Rose arrived with Professor Copeland. Several fathers rolled up, and a man to deliver some garden furniture.

'It's my special offer,' said Rose excitedly. 'We must hide it in the cellar before Ace arrives.' Berenice had decided to give up grumbling about her belt and had found a soulmate in Delphinium.

'It's hard to keep your mind alive when you spend your time with people three feet high,' she was saying.

I looked at my watch. It was five o'clock and the conjuror was quarter of an hour late. I mopped my brow; we'd have to eat soon.

There was a howl as Damian, whose blindfold seemed to have slipped, plunged the donkey's tail into Professor Copeland's bottom. Midas was hitting Jason over the head with a tennis racket still in its press.

'I shouldn't engage in that form of activity if I were you, Midas,' said Delphinium.

'It's amazing,' said Berenice, 'the way children work out their hostility if you don't interfere with their natural instincts.'

Five-fifteen, still no conjuror. I shepherded all the children into the kitchen for tea.

'What's this crap?' said Damian, picking up a piece of carrot cake and hurling it at Jason.

'Crap,' said Midas, picking up a soya bean canape and hurling it at Antonia Fraser.

Two of the Pollys or Emilies or Sophies started to cry.

'Aren't they a nightmare?' said Maggie, putting her head round the door.

'Why doesn't Delphinium do anything to control them?' I said in desperation.

'She lives in a Commune on the other side of Windermere. I don't think she's very into discipline. Their father commutes to London in a Ferrari,' said Maggie.

The conjuror, a pouf with brushed forward hair, finally arrived gibbering with guilt and ill temper at 5.30. Talk about the panic stations of the extremely cross. 'The roads are simply atrocious. I'd like to get started straight away,' he said.

And by some miracle, five minutes later he had all the children sitting spellbound at his feet in the study, and pigeons coming out of his sleeve.

Phew: Blissful relief! The grown-ups were having a rip-roaring party in the drawing-room; everyone was well away. I was just pouring myself and Mrs. Braddock a drink when the door bell rang yet again.

'I always read Rod McKuen to my potted plants,' Berenice was saying.

As no one was obviously going to move, I went to answer the door.

It was another mother. She had bruised eyes, ash blonde hair and the startled look of a race horse. She was also vaguely familiar.

'Hullo,' she said nervously. 'Is it all right if I come in?'

'Of course,' I said. 'If you've come to collect, I'm afraid we're running behind schedule. The conjuror arrived late, but the grown-ups are having a terrific party in the drawing-room. You know what the Mulhollands are like!'

She smiled. 'Only too well! I'm Fay.'

I swallowed. 'Oh, my goodness. I'm Pru.' What on earth was Maggie going to say?

'Lucasta's talked about you on the telephone,' she said. 'You've been so kind to her. Are you sure it's all right my coming?'

She was so friendly, you couldn't not like her.

'Of course it is. How was the play?'

'It was good,' she said, taking off a rather worn fur coat. 'I had a nice director, I think he'll give me more work. Has Lucasta had a nice birthday?'

'Sensational,' I shouted over the party roar as we passed at the drawing-room door.

'Gosh, I'm nervous of going in there,' said Fay.

She needn't have been. Rose gave a shriek of excitement and fell on her neck.

'Darling, darling Fay,' she cried. 'How lovely to see you! You shouldn't have stayed away so long, and how ravishing you look. You've lost so much weight. How lovely. James! Berenice! Delphinium! This is Fay, Jack's first wife, and Lucasta's mother.'

Everyone crowded round Fay, saying how nice it was to see her again.

'I'm Ivan's permanent commitment,' I heard Berenice saying.

Suddenly I caught a glimpse of Maggie's face through the throng. I felt sick; she looked absolutely crucified. I was about to fight my way through to her when I heard a scream. In the hall I found the conjuror in floods of tears.

'They're the worst lot of kids I've ever had to deal with. They're little monsters. That Damian tried to send one of my pigeons up the chimney with a message for Santa Claus and singed all its feathers.' He wiped his eyes. 'I can't go on.'

'Oh please,' I said. 'You were booked for an hour. Have a strong drink and another go.'

'I don't drink,' sobbed the conjuror, 'and you need a body-guard for that lot. Leave that rabbit alone, you little sod,' he screamed, rushing back into the study.

Jack was next to arrive. He was in a good temper. He'd pulled off a terrific deal with the Americans.

'Maggie and I can spend Christmas in Bermuda if we want to.'

'I'm not sure *she'll* want to,' I said, 'Fay's in the drawing-room, being fêted by everyone.'

Jack's face lit up : 'Fay is? Isn't she great? I must go and say hullo.'

Damian burst out of the study and ran yelling down the passage towards the kitchen.

'Beautiful child, isn't he?' I said sourly.

'Probably mine,' said Jack.

'He's a monster,' I protested. 'He belongs to someone called Delphinium.'

Jack laughed. 'Then he's definitely mine.'

He smoothed his hair in the hall mirror, straightened his tie, and fought his way into the drawing-room.

'Look who's here, Jack darling,' I heard Rose shriek. 'It's darling Fay. Doesn't she look beautiful?'

The next moment Maggie came out of the room. I caught a glimpse of her white stricken face as she fled upstairs.

After that the party got completely out of hand. The children came screaming out of the study, followed by the conjuror still in tears.

'I want my money,' he said, 'and I'm going.'

No one of course had any cash. Jack had an Irish 50p, and Berenice had travellers' cheques, and the conjuror wouldn't take an ordinary cheque.

'I want cash on delivery,' he said, firmly sitting down on his trunk of magic. 'I don't trust that lot in there not to bounce cheques, and I'm going to wait until I get it.'

I could just have paid him myself but I wanted to keep enough cash for my fare back to London – just in case.

In the drawing-room Jack was chatting to Fay, one hand holding a drink, the other lying along the sofa behind her head. He looked the picture of handsome relaxed contentment.

Berenice surprisingly was nose to nose with Professor Copeland. 'I think it's so terrific,' she was saying, 'how you're able to plug into yourself and find this conduit into your unconscious and be able to tap all that energy.'

Rose was suddenly looking a little disconsolate.

Jason ran screaming through the crowd, followed by Damian and Midas, each carrying one of Jack's Masai spears. The Professor and Berenice followed their progress fondly.

'If I'd been able to act out what I felt like that, I'm sure I wouldn't have had to spend all those years in analysis,' said the Professor. 'I mean my father's a case-book example of an anal retentive.'

'You're working too hard. Come and sit down and talk to Fay,' Jack shouted across at me.

'I will in a minute.' I said.

In the kitchen I found Coleridge and Wordsworth and Antonia Fraser and the kitten demolishing the food. But even they drew the line at lentil loaf and carrot cake. Upstairs I found Maggie a sodden, heaving lump on her bed.

'I can't bear it, I can't bear it. I expected her to look like an old frump,' she sobbed, 'and she turns up looking gorgeous, and Jack's obviously mad about her. She must have been on a diet for days. I never thought she'd be that thin. And everyone's w-watching and saying how much prettier she is than me.'

'Of course they're not,' I said firmly. 'You're much prettier than she is, and *much* younger.'

'Look how they're all over her, Jack, Berenice, Copeland, Rose, even Ace I expect when he gets back. They're so fickle.'

'They want to make things easier for Lucasta,' I said. 'And I expect Jack feels guilty because he left her for you, and he wants to make things up to her, not to go back at all, just to say he's sorry.'

'I hate them; I hate them both,' sobbed Maggie.

More screams downstairs, and a volley of loud explosions. 'I'll be back in a minute,' I said.

Damian and Midas were standing on the stairs. They had found a packet of cigarettes, and had lit up and were systematically bursting balloons.

'Stop it,' I screamed. They took no notice. They really ought to join some para-military operation like the Scouts.

More dads arrived in second cars to collect children and mums who were not sober enough to drive, and they all stayed for the party, and had to be got drinks as well.

Lucasta was sitting on Jack's knee now, playing with Fay's charm bracelet. They all looked so happy. Jesus, I thought, what a bloody lot of unhappiness divorce makes.

Professor Copeland and Berenice were still having a great rap. 'I found I couldn't write about it,' she was saying. 'My life with Aaron was too painful to be transformed into enduring art.'

'Don't pull Antonia Fraser's tail like that, Damian,' said Delphinium. 'Physical violence is not the answer.'

'Perhaps I will have a drink after all,' said the conjuror.

Somewhere in the distance I heard the back door slam. It was seven o'clock now. I was worried about Ace. The roads must be like glass.

'When we give a children's party,' said Berenice, 'we just write the scenario as we go along.'

In the hall, Damian and Midas were writing their own scenario in red lipstick all over the walls.

'Stop it!' I screamed at them. 'Stop it, you little monsters!'

Once again neither of them took any notice. Then Damian raised two fingers at me.

The next moment Jason came out of the kitchen brandishing a kitchen knife.

'No,' I shrieked.

A key turned in the door and Ace walked in. Oh the blissful, blissful relief to see him.

'Oh, thank God you've come,' I said.

'What's the matter?'

'They are.' I pointed to Damian and Midas, and Jason who was now deciding which to carve up.

Ace was across the room in a flash.

'Stop it,' he said firmly, removing Jason's knife, and picking both Damian and Midas up by the scruff of the neck, 'or I'll bash all your heads together. There's a television in the study. Go and watch it.'

To my amazement they went quietly.

'What else is the matter?'

'The conjuror's in hysterics. He couldn't handle the

173

children, and no one's got enough money to pay him, so he's joined the party and started drinking, and he doesn't drink.'

'Go and get him.' said Ace, getting a wad of tenners out of his notecase.

'What else?' he said, after the conjuror had been dispatched into the night.

'Fay's here,' I said miserably. 'Rose is all over her, and Jack's flirting like mad with her.'

'And Maggie?' he said swiftly. He always got the point at once.

'She's in absolute floods upstairs.'

He went towards the stairs. 'I'll go up and talk to her. Be an angel and mix me a very stiff whisky.'

'Was it all right today?' I said. 'Not too awful?'

He shrugged his shoulders. 'Pretty bloody, but at least it's done.'

I went into the drawing-room to get the whisky. The party showed no signs of abating at all.

'Where's Ivan?' said Berenice. 'He should be back by now.'

'He's back,' I said. 'He's upstairs with Maggie.'

Berenice's eyes narrowed till they seemed one black slit across her face.

'She's upset,' I explained.

'Whatever for?'

'She's unhappy because Fay's here.'

'She's so old-fashioned,' said Berenice scornfully. 'Everyone's loose about exes these days; it's healthy; you've got to stay loose. I can't understand jealousy, it's something I've never suffered from.'

'Oh I'm sure you're above that sort of thing,' I snapped.

I put some ice in the whisky and shot out of the room.

I met Ace coming down the stairs; he looked very bleak; he was holding a letter.

'What's the matter?' I said.

'Maggie's walked out.'

'To Pendle?' I whispered.

'So she says in this note to Jack.' He put his hand on my arm. 'I'm sorry.'

174

'Oh God, how awful. But she can't have got far; she was here twenty minutes ago.'

He opened the front door and looked out – snow was eddying and whirling and a shower of hard tiny frozen flakes swept inside.

'Jack's car's gone. She must have taken it. Must be trying for the 7.45. She could kill herself on these roads.'

Suddenly he looked ashen beneath his suntan. He must be remembering Elizabeth driving too fast on icy roads in her excitement to meet him at the airport. He took the whisky from me and drained it in one gulp.

'I'm going to see if I can stop her. Don't say anything until I've got back – say I've gone to get some cigarettes.'

He was back in three-quarters of an hour.

'I just missed her. She left the car parked across the road – as a final gesture of defiance, I suppose. I'd better go and break up the party.'

We went into the drawing-room.

'Ivan, sweetest.' Berenice extracted herself from Professor Copeland and a ring of fathers and, crossing the room, put her arms round Ace's neck and kissed him tenderly. 'Where have you been?'

The nannies perked up and pulled down their sweaters, the mothers patted their hair. Even pale and travel-worn, Ace was still a knock-out. I wondered why I hadn't noticed it when I first met him.

He went over and kissed Fay who was still thigh to thigh with Jack on the sofa.

'Hullo, my love, you're looking very beautiful,' he said. 'I'm glad about the play.'

Her eyes lit up. 'Goodness, it's lovely to see you. How was America? Very successful obviously. I'm so pleased about you and Berenice.' She lowered her voice. 'I meant to write about Elizabeth, but I wasn't very together at the time.'

It must have been just after Jack left her. Perhaps, now Maggie had gone, they might get together again.

Ace, however, had other ideas.

'I thought you might like a lift home.'

'She's staying for supper,' said Jack quickly.

'Anyway, the party's not over,' cried Rose.

'It'd be better if she came another day,' said Ace firmly. 'Lucasta's tired. And it's high time these children went home.'

Over by the window Damian and Midas were systematically cramming a plate of meringues down Jason's velvet suit.

Somehow Ace managed to empty the room in ten minutes. I went upstairs with Fay and helped pack Lucasta's things and gather up her presents.

'I've got a tummy egg,' wailed Lucasta.

'You've been eating too many sweets,' said Fay.

As we went downstairs Jack was saying angrily to Ace, 'What the bloody hell's going on? Why can't Fay stay for supper? We can't throw her out on a night like this.'

Ace got Maggie's letter out of his pocket. 'I think you'd better read this,' he said grimly.

As he and Jack went into the drawing-room, he turned to me : 'Can you say goodbye to Fay and Lucasta for us?'

Outside Lucasta hugged me tightly.

'Can I come and stay with you in London? Will you take me to see the knife guards at Buckingham Palace?'

'Of course I will,' I said, clinging to her. I couldn't bear to let her go.

'Was Ace shocked that I was here?' whispered Fay anxiously.

'No, it was Maggie. She was a bit jealous.'

'*She* was jealous?' said Fay with sudden bitterness. 'It was she who took him away from me in the first place. I suppose it was tactless of me to stay. I was so pleased to see them all again,' she added wistfully. 'They're so lovely.'

'I know they are,' I said.

I went back into the house, pausing to look at my pale reflection in the looking glass in the hall. I still only had one eye made up. The drawing-room door was open.

'Pru,' Rose called, 'we're all in here.'

Jack was sitting on the window seat, surrounded by a debris of crisps, coloured streamers and burst balloons. Upon his face was a desolation so haggard I hardly recognized him. Berenice had her supportive face on. Ace handed me a stiff gin and tonic. Rose was revelling in the situation.

'Isn't it dreadful?' she said to me. 'Maggie and I were playing bridge tomorrow, and she's taken Professor Copeland's hat with her.'

'And my Hermes belt I shouldn't wonder,' said Berenice.

'It's very odd of Maggie,' said Rose. 'I thought Pendle was supposed to be Pru's boyfriend.'

Jack turned to me. 'You saw her last. What did she say?'

'I think she was jealous of you chatting up Fay. She'd never met her before. She was – well – a bit shocked Fay looked so attractive, and you seemed so pleased to see her.'

'Hell, I *was* pleased to see her,' said Jack. 'I always liked her when we weren't rowing.'

'I take saunas with my ex and his permanent commitment,' said Berenice. 'You've gotta stay loose about exes.'

Jack shot her a look of pure hatred; then he turned to Ace.

'I can't believe she's gone. Shall I drive down and get her?'

Ace shook his head. 'Leave her alone. If you drag her away now, she'll never know how much she hated living with Pen.'

'She might like it.'

'They'll drive each other round the bend.'

Jack looked at his untouched drink. 'I deserve it, I suppose. I had absolutely no compunction about pinching her from Pen in the first place. It's an eye for an eye.' He gave a hollow laugh. 'At least she won't have to change her name.'

'Oh let her go, Jack,' said Rose. 'She's not worth bothering about.'

It was the first time I'd seen Jack angry – it was terrifying.

'Shut up! you stupid bitch,' he spat at Rose. 'If it hadn't been for you leading her astray . . .'

Rose bridled. 'Really Jack. There's no need to speak to your mother like that.'

Ace took Rose's arm. 'Why don't you watch television?'

Rose tossed her head. 'Do you really think I'd watch television at a time like this?'

'Go on !' said Ace. She flounced out.

Ace turned to Berenice and me. 'Can you both possibly keep her happy for half-an-hour?'

We found Rose thumbing through the *Radio Times* in the study.

'We had a really good bridge four lined up,' she said. 'Maggie might have waited until Wednesday. She never had any sense of proportion.'

I wasn't listening. I was thinking about Ace.

'Charlie Drake's on in a minute,' said Rose suddenly. 'Switch it on, there's a love. I've just got time to go and tell the Professor about Maggie. He won't be at all pleased about his hat.'

She bustled out into the hall. Antonia Fraser was sharpening her claws on the sofa. The television leapt noisily into life. Reginald Bosanquet was talking about the chaos caused on the roads by the snow.

'British news is so parochial,' said Berenice, turning it down. 'You must be upset, Prudence,' she went on. 'You won't get your lift back to London now.'

'Oh shut up,' I said.

Berenice picked at the polish on one of her long scarlet nails.

'You only hurt yourself by coming on hostile,' she said. 'Don't you realize anger is just the flipside of depression? You must ask yourself why you feel threatened by me.'

'I can't stand your crummy philosophizing.'

'You're not being honest, Prudence. There's a time when absolute honesty must take precedence in an enlightened community over more pragmatic considerations. Otherwise we simply re-create the hypocrisy of our times.'

'Could I have an interpreter?' I said, taking a slug of my gin.

'You're emotionally fixated on Ivan.'

'I am *not* !' But I could feel myself going scarlet.

'Oh yes, and he knows it too – and he's very, very embarrassed by it.'

178

'Can't imagine him being embarrassed by anything,' I said.

'That shows how untuned you are into other people's vibrations. Ivan's been supportive to you over the past week or so because you've been ill, and he thought Pendle gave you a raw deal. He cares about people, he's a people person.'

'Hold on while I rummage for my sick bag,' I said desperately.

'Prudence, don't joke about this. Everyone is embarrassed by you being here, but they expected Pendle would be here tomorrow to take you back. Now it's quite obvious Pendle's cashed in his chips where you're concerned, do you honestly want to go on outstaying your welcome?'

'No,' I whispered. 'No, of course I don't.'

'Ivan's got enough worries coping with Jack and Rose. He doesn't need you hanging around like a lovesick teeny-bopper anymore, playing gooseberry.'

Reginald Bosanquet was making a little end-of-programme joke with Andrew Gardner about a canary who'd learned to whistle Beethoven's Ninth.

Rose bustled in full of excitement. 'The Professor's going to send Pendle a bill for that hat. It cost £50 at Herbert Johnson.'

'Rose,' I said, 'would you mind awfully if I slipped off to bed? I'm still a bit weak, and it's been rather an exhausting day.'

I slunk into bed, clutching the kitten, and turned off the light. Tomorrow I'd beat it. I wasn't hanging around any longer being a nuisance.

Hours and hours later, I heard Ace and Jack coming to bed, still talking in low voices.

CHAPTER SIXTEEN

ACE came in to see me very early next morning and handed me a letter from Jane.

'I'm going into Manchester with Jack to see our solicitor,' he said. 'I'll be back for lunch. You don't look too good. Yesterday must have tired you out. Don't get up till I get back.'

He ran a finger down my cheek. 'I'm sorry a family crisis has blown up in your face.'

He's going, I thought in panic, trying to imprint his features on my memory, and I'll never see him again. It was as though my heart was being torn out of me. As he reached the door, I called to him.

'Thank you for looking after me and everything.'

He turned. 'I haven't finished yet.'

'I'm sorry I've been difficult.'

His face softened. 'You've been bloody difficult.' And he was gone.

I dressed quickly, flinging my clothes into a suitcase, and then went to see Rose, who was horrified at being woken at such an ungodly hour.

'I've just had a letter from my mother,' I lied. 'She's awfully ill, and there's no one to look after my father, so I'm afraid I shall have to leave at once.'

'Oh dear,' said Rose petulantly. 'Everyone's going. First Pendle, then Jimmy, then Maggie, and now you. It's like something out of Chekhov. Never mind. You must come again. Braddock will drive you to the station.'

'Would you mind if I took the kitten?' I said.

'Of course not,' said Rose. 'Far too many animals around the place as it is. We might have a basket somewhere.'

My letter to Ace took ages. It's so difficult when all you want to say to someone is, 'I love you, I love you, I love you.' In the end it was a bald little note saying thank you and that my mother was ill.

Mr. Braddock put my things in the car. The kitten was thumping round in its basket, mewing piteously. I went into the kitchen. Berenice was sitting eating her revolting rats'-dropping-in-sawdust breakfast, and reading the *Guardian*. I ignored her and hugged Mrs. Braddock.

'Goodbye, and thank you for bringing up all those trays and everything.'

Mrs. Braddock mopped her eyes with her apron.

'You're a good girl and you worked very hard yesterday. And we'll all miss you very much. I hope you come again soon, although I'm not sure I'll be here.' She shot a venemous glance at Berenice, who calmly went on eating.

Mr. Braddock appeared in the doorway. 'We'll have to hurry, love, if we're going to catch the train.'

I walked to the door, ignoring Berenice, but she looked up and said :

'Goodbye Prudence, I'm sure you'll find a permanent commitment soon. I hope you've got enough ego strength not to take Ivan's rejection as a sign of rejection.'

For a second I looked at her meditatively, teeny bopper to woman. Then I said, 'As you keep saying, the only really authentic thing in life is to act on your own impulses.' And I picked up her plate of horrible health food and emptied it, milk and all, over her shiny newly washed head. 'And I'll come and throw brown rice at your wedding,' I added. Then I ran out to the waiting car.

Rose was waiting outside. It was a beautiful day. The sunshine, the sparkling snow and the rollicking dogs seemed so incongruous beside my black suicidal gloom.

'Goodbye Rose darling,' I said, leaping into the car. 'Give my love to Jack – and Ace.'

As she waved me off, I felt like a barnacle being prised away from its rock.

The mountains gleamed like marble against the bright

blue sky, snow ivied the walls, every twig and grass blade glittered thickly like sparkler fireworks. What was the poem we learnt at school?

> 'Crack goes the whip, and off we go.
> The trees and houses smaller grow.
> Last, round the woody turn we swing.
> Goodbye, goodbye to everything.'

I turned and caught a last glimpse of the Mulhollands' house with its dark fringe of pines. I felt I must be leaving behind a shiny snail's mark of tears.

Suddenly I heard a low chuckle. I looked at Mr. Braddock's impassive face; then he chuckled again.

'Mrs. Braddock and I could scarcely restrain ourselves,' he said. 'We could have cheered and cheered. To my dying day I shall remember the expression on her face with all the milk and stuff dripping down it. I wish I had the nerve to do something like that. Anyway your name shall be writ large for evermore.'

'Oh dear, I could do without the publicity. Ace is going to be livid.'

'Perhaps it will make the scales fall from his eyes. If that woman becomes mistress of Ambleside, Mrs. Braddock and I will be out on our ears.'

Then he chuckled again.

After buying a platform ticket and carrying my suitcase and the still furiously mewing kitten on to the platform, he said he'd be off. 'I've got a lot of snow to shovel, but perhaps I may shake you by the hand.'

'Pleased I've made someone happy,' I said, gloomily.

The journey back to London was a nightmare. Tears kept trickling out from under my dark glasses. The train was packed, and all the old ladies who said how sweet the kitten was when I got into the carriage and begged me to let him out of his basket, got fed up when he crawled all over them and laddered their stockings. I commuted between the loos all down the train, crying myself stupid until someone rattled the door, then moving on to the next one.

Jane was obviously not expecting me back for ages. She was out, and she'd been making full use of my wardrobe. My clothes were strewn all over the bedroom, and she'd left the top off my favourite bottle of scent. I made the kitten at home, gave it a tin of lobster we had in the larder, and wandered desolately round the flat wondering if I'd been crazy to walk out like that.

Jane came in about ten, and made a great fuss about being pleased to see me. She was horribly embarrassed, because she was wearing my fur coat and my boots. Suddenly she looked at me for the first time full in the face. Her embarrassment turned to horror.

'Pru, lovie, you look like a road accident. What, or rather who, have you been up to?'

'I've been ill,' I said, and burst into tears. Eventually, the whole story came pouring out.

'I knew all along, of course,' said Jane sententiously. 'I could tell from your letter you were getting over Pendle pretty quickly, and there was an obvious swing towards Ace.

'Mind you, I think you're raving mad,' she went on. 'I wouldn't have left. I'd have battled it out with this Berenice woman – what a soppy name! Look how keen on Pendle you were, and now look at you. Well, Ace may have fancied this woman a bit, and now he doesn't. You wait, he'll come pounding after you.'

But Ace didn't come after me. For the first time in my life, I became familiar with real hell. You don't need a pitchfork and demons, just take someone away from someone they love – that's enough. Before, when I'd been unhappily in love, it only needed a handsome man giving me the glad eye in the street, or a patch of blue sky above a grey building to jerk me temporarily out of my gloom. But this time it was unrelieved despair. I dragged myself round the flat like a wounded animal and every night I cried great earth-shaking sobs until dawn came.

The weekend crawled by – not a letter, not a telephone

call. I even rang up the engineers to check if the telephone was working. Jane, worried at first, got rather fed up with me. One can't dole out sympathy indefinitely. She rang Rodney, who took her out for a long drunken Sunday lunch to discuss what to do for and about Prudence.

On Monday morning, back in the office, gazing at a lot of statistics about canned peaches, I was just wondering how I'd ever get through the week when the telephone rang. Rodney answered it.

'It's for you,' he said, waving the receiver. 'A voice from your immediate past.'

'Who is it?' I said listlessly.

'Someone called Mulholland.'

I was across the room like a streak of light.

'Hullo, Pru,' said a familiar drawling voice. It was Maggie.

'How are you?' I said, battling with my disappointment.

'Comme ci, Comme very ca. Pendle's out. Come to lunch.'

'I'd like to,' I said. Crazy masochist, I couldn't resist talking to someone who knew Ace, and I was also curious to know how she was enjoying living with Pendle.

When I arrived, I hardly recognized Pendle's flat. It had always been so impeccably tidy. Now clothes lay everywhere, carrier bags and tissue paper were littered all over the floor. Ashtrays were overflowing, and Maggie had made dramatic inroads into that well-stocked drinks cupboard. Professor Copeland's hat, still carrying a fair sprinkling of Antonia Fraser's ginger hairs, was perched rakishly over the nose of Julius Caesar's bust.

She hugged me when I arrived. 'Pru, how lovely to see you! I rang quite on the off-chance. I thought you might still be at home. Are you wildly hungry?'

I shook my head.

'Good, because I'm afraid we've only got whisky and some smoked salmon for lunch.'

She poured us out huge drinks.

'Do you like my new kit?' she asked, twirling round. She was wearing a red midi dress, and her hair was permed into tight little curls. She'd plucked her eyebrows to the edge of extinction, and was wearing pink shoes.

'Super,' I said. I thought she looked frightful.

'I'm as "in" as you are now. I came away without any luggage so Pendle had to buy me a new wardrobe. We've been out every night, plays and films and nightclubs. We went to Hester's last night. Have you ever been there?'

I shook my head.

'Pendle's wonderful. He does everything to keep me amused. Do you know what he said to me as soon as I got here? "Please unpack, darling – everything – then I can get rid of your suitcase," and then, towards the end of the first night – neither of us slept a wink – he said, "This is the happiest night of my life, better than when I passed my Bar finals, or got that scholarship to Oxford." The awful thing is, having longed for me to come and live with him for so long, I don't think he quite knows what to do with me.' She rattled on feverishly.

Then suddenly, as she was casually shaking ice around in her glass, she said, 'How was Jack when I left? Did he mind?'

'Yes, he did, he minded like hell. He nearly murdered Rose when she said he was better off without you. He loves you. He was simply shattered. He couldn't stop looking at your photograph and saying he couldn't believe it.'

She went over to the record-player. 'Pendle has such ghastly records. I went and bought some pop ones, but I've played them into the ground.'

She swung round. Her eyes were full of tears. 'Was Jack really upset?'

'Yes.'

'Then why didn't he come and get me?'

'He wanted to, but Ace wouldn't let him. Ace said it would be better if you realized you didn't like living with Pendle first.'

Maggie put her face in her hands. 'Ace is quite right, blast him!' she said. 'I always thought Pendle was much more interesting and enigmatic than Jack. But he isn't. He's just boring. Jack's much funnier, and he never minded me being a slut; he just roared with laughter. If only he didn't run after other women so much.'

'He doesn't mean anything by it,' I said. 'He's just proving that he's attractive, like gorillas beat their chests.'

'And, what's more, I think I'm pregnant and it's Jack's child and Pendle wants me to have an abortion.'

'Oh, you can't.'

'I know. I've had a lot of time to think about Jack, and I think if we were away from Rose with a house and baby of our own we might get it together.'

'What are you going to do?'

Maggie got up and picked up one of her new dresses, and held it against her. 'I don't know. Do you think I can take these new clothes with me?'

She looked at my untouched smoked salmon.

'You're not eating anything – you look ghastly.'

'Thanks!' I said.

'It's Ace, I suppose.'

'What do you mean?' I stammered, my mouth full of ashes.

'All that bull about hating his guts. It stood out as plain as a spot on one's nose that you were hooked on him.'

'How?' I said.

'You never addressed a civil word to him, and the way you were always going on about him not being attractive. It's like saying grass is red.'

'Anyway,' I said wearily, 'it doesn't matter what *I* feel. He's going to marry Berenice.'

'Of course he won't,' said Maggie scornfully, 'Jack reckons Ace is hooked on you too. All that little Hitler behaviour when you were ill, and that's why he was so stroppy when Berenice turned up and put a spoke in the wheel. I mean, he couldn't just throw her out the moment she arrived. They *had* been living together in New York. Oh

186

look, you've spilt your drink all over the carpet.' She mopped
it up with one of Pendle's silk cushions.

'Do you really think he won't marry her?'

'Not in a million years. Do you really think Jack was
missing me?'

CHAPTER SEVENTEEN

DURING the afternoon, my elation subsided. If Ace had been keen on me, he would have contacted me by now. I felt completely exhausted when I got back to the flat.

Jane was eating bread and jam with one hand and trying to put in heated rollers with the other.

'Where are you going?' I asked.

'Out with Rodney,' she said.

'Again?' I said in disgust.

'We've decided what's the matter with you,' she said. 'You're suffering from the Dr. Kildare syndrome.'

'Oh yeah?'

'Well, you know women always fall in love with their gynaecologists, and their doctor. It's the same with you. Ace looked after you when you were ill so you see him as your doctor. You'll find you get over him very quickly.'

'Very clever!' I snapped.

'And, by the way, Pendle's on his way round.'

'That's all I need,' I groaned. 'I only hope Maggie hasn't left him already. What on earth can he want? Have we got any drink?'

'Only some cooking sherry.'

'I'll pop round to the off-licence and get some,' I said.

'I'd forgotten what a marvellously sexy voice he's got,' said Jane.

I caught a glance of myself in the off-licence mirror. I looked ghastly – like an Oxfam advertisement. I wondered dolefully if I'd ever be pretty again. I walked home past the pet shop, listlessly looking at the notices on the door : 'Please remove your crash helmet before entering, it frightens the parrot.' 'Due to bereavement will someone provide a home for Fluff, a black and white Tom? Fluff is lovable and clean'. Oh dear, due to bereavement will someone provide a home for Prudence, quite clean but not very lovable? If I don't tread on any of the lines on the way home, I said to myself, I'll get over Ace. And off I went, taking longer and longer strides and then a string of little ones. Then I spoilt it all by bumping into a lamp-post and treading on three lines at once. I let myself into the flat.

'Hullo' I shouted. Jane came into the hall, making an agonized face and pointed at the drawing-room door.

Steeling myself, I went in. I felt the blood drain out of me. I clutched the table for support. Standing with his back to the fire, like a great mountain, was Ace.

'What on earth are you doing here?' I stammered. 'Jane said Pendle was coming round.'

'She got the wrong Mulholland,' he said. 'We sound the same on the telephone.' He looked desperately tired and there were huge black rings under his eyes.

'I've missed you,' he said, and if it hadn't been Ace, and he hadn't been sun-tanned, I could have sworn he was blushing. 'I've missed you like hell.'

He held out his arms and I went straight into them. I thought he would kiss all the life out of me.

Then he said, 'Why the bloody hell did you run off like that?' which sounded more like the old Ace.

'How did you find me?' I said.

'A damned dance you've led me with that cock-and-bull story about your mother being ill. After hunting through every telephone directory the Post Office had to offer, I finally found your parents' number. Your mother must have thought I was mad when I said I was sorry she was sick. However, we had an illuminating little chat. She said she hadn't heard from you for ages, but she'd gathered from your flatmate that you were staying with some "very odd" people in the North of England.'

I scuffed the carpet with my foot.

'I thought you were going to marry Berenice.' I said.

'What on earth gave you that idea?'

'Berenice did.'

'She would,' said Ace. 'She doesn't think so now. She's not very pleased with you either, wantonly emptying breakfast food over her newly washed hair. Think of all the starving health-food freaks in Russia.'

I hung my head. Then I saw that he was laughing.

'But I saw Maggie today,' I said quickly, 'and she said you weren't going to marry her.'

'I know you saw Maggie,' he said. 'I talked to her on the telephone before I came round here. I derived a certain amount of comfort from the fact that she said you were looking like death.'

'How's Jack?' I asked.

'Pretty low – but Maggie'd better pull her finger out if she wants to go back to him. He was beginning to chat up one of the better-looking Nannies who came to Lucasta's party when I left.'

I giggled. 'He is awful.'

'He's just Jack,' said Ace.

'D'you think Maggie will go back?' I asked.

'Frankly, I couldn't care less at the moment. All I know is that Professor Copeland broke his toe on a stone hot water-bottle creeping into Rose's bed last night, and hasn't stopped complaining since and I am sick to death of other people's problems. I'm far more interested in my own. Pru, look at me.'

I was almost blinded by the blaze of love in his eyes.

'I love you,' he said simply, 'to total distraction. You slunk into my heart, snapping and snarling like a vixen, so I didn't realize it was happening – but I think I really began loving you the first moment I saw you.'

'But you were so nasty to me,' I said in amazement. 'I thought you thought I was awful. Did you really fancy me?'

'Yes, to use your revolting expression, I did "fancy" you, even during the row we had after the firework party. My God,' he added, coming towards me and taking my hands, 'if you had any idea of the self-control I've had to exert, all the time you were in bed at home, and that day by the sea. I

190

was so nervous of making a false move, I was proceeding like a batsman on 99, but I was all set to declare myself that evening. Then Jimmy Batten and Berenice arrived, and suddenly I thought you were still hooked on Pendle.'

'I wasn't,' I said, 'I was just trying to hide the fact that I was bananas about you.'

'Jesus,' said Ace, 'we have wasted a lot of time.'

'D'you want a drink?'

'Not yet,' he said, sitting down in the armchair and pulling me on to his knee.

'About Berenice,' I muttered.

Ace sighed. 'I was certainly screwing her in New York. I was lonely – still missing Elizabeth. I've never been very good at playing the field. She was a big star. I suppose I was flattered, but she certainly didn't travel to England.'

'And there was her superior muscle tone, Ivan,' I said, innocently.

'Shut up' said Ace, pulling one of my curls. 'You can take the piss out of me after we're married but not before.'

I went very still.

'What about Elizabeth?'

'I loved Lizzie; nothing can take that away.'

'I wouldn't want to,' I said quickly.

'But it doesn't hurt anymore since I met you. That day I went to see her parents, I kept wishing you were there to cheer everything up. In the end I found myself telling them all about you, that I loved you.'

'Oh, goodness. Were they upset?'

'They understood. They said they'd like to meet you next time you come up.'

His hands tightened on mine. 'I want you, Pru – for good.'

I still couldn't take it in. I felt dizzy and had to get up and take a turn round the room.

'But you don't understand,' I said in agitation. 'I'm a belligerent scruff, and I'm scatty, and I'd shipwreck your smart dinner parties and upset all your grand friends.'

He pulled me back on to his knee, and putting his arms around me, said very gently, 'Darling, stop jibbering. Do I have to spell it out for you? Isn't it enough that you're beautiful, and funny and you make me happy — and just holding you in my arms gives me the first peace I've had in days?'

He looked at me for a minute and then bent his head and kissed me until I thought I'd faint with excitement.

'Don't you think, in my turn,' he said, 'I'm terrified that I'm ten years older than you and that I've got a frightful reputation for being difficult and a bully?'

'Who said so?' I asked furiously. 'How dare they!'

'You did,' he said, examining his finger-nails. 'And it's also a slight bother that you haven't told me yet that you love me.'

'Oh,' I cried in horror, 'Oh, darling, darling Ace, don't you understand that I'm absolutely, deliriously bonkers out of my mind for you? It was the same with me. I think I was hooked on you from the first moment I saw you. I've never reacted so violently to anyone in my life. I've been so desperately unhappy since Berenice arrived, and even worse since I left you — and now you're here, I can't quite take it in. It's just like discovering Father Christmas is real after all.' I was crawling all over him like a kitten, and kissing him.

His hand tightened on my shoulder. His face was expressionless, but I knew he was pleased. With his other hand he held out an imaginary microphone to me.

'Well,' he said, putting on a toneless, carefully modulated television announcer's voice, 'I'm sure everyone looking in was fascinated by that lucid dissertation on love, I know I was. But I'm afraid time's running out. In the few seconds we have left, would you mind very quickly summing up your views on marriage?'

I gave a sigh of happiness, 'Oh, yes, I would. Oh yes, please,' I said.

THE END

EMILY BY JILLY COOPER

If Emily hadn't gone to Annie Richmond's party, she would never have met the impossible, irresistible Rory Balniel – never have married him and been carried off to the wild Scottish island of Irasa to live in his ancestral home along with his eccentric mother Coco, and the dog, Walter Scott. She'd never have met the wild and mysterious Marina, a wraith from Rory's past, nor her brother, the disagreeable Finn Maclean; never have spent a night in a haunted highland castle, or been caught stealing roses in a see-through nightie . . . Yes, it all started at Annie Richmond's party . . .

'EMILY opens windows on to a new romantic landscape . . . The young and young-in-heart will revel in it.'

Newsagent and Bookshop

0 552 10277 6

BELLA BY JILLY COOPER

There was no doubt Bella Parkinson was a success: the most promising actress in London, bright, sexy – and hopelessly scatter-brained – she was taking the town by storm. Rupert Henriques, dashingly handsome and wealthy enough to buy her every theatre in London if she wanted it, couldn't wait to marry her . . .

But Bella had a secret in her past – and the one man who knew it was about to come into her life again . . . Rupert's sinister cousin Lazlo, for some reason of his own, was trying to prevent her marriage. Before she knew where she was, Bella found herself in real danger . . .

0 552 10427 2

OTHER JILLY COOPER TITLES AVAILABLE FROM CORGI BOOKS

THE PRICES SHOWN BELOW WERE CORRECT AT THE TIME OF GOING TO PRESS. HOWEVER TRANSWORLD PUBLISHERS RESERVE THE RIGHT TO SHOW NEW RETAIL PRICES ON COVERS WHICH MAY DIFFER FROM THOSE PREVIOUSLY ADVERTISED IN THE TEXT OR ELSEWHERE.

☐	10427 2	**Bella**	£2.99
☐	10277 6	**Emily**	£2.99
☐	10576 7	**Harriet**	£2.99
☐	11149 x	**Imogen**	£2.99
☐	12041 3	**Lisa & Co.**	£2.99
☐	10717 4	**Octavia**	£2.99
☐	12486 9	**Riders**	£4.99
☐	11525 8	**Class**	£3.99
☐	13264 0	**Rivals**	£4.99

All Corgi/Bantam Books are available at your bookshop or newsagent, or can be ordered from the following address:
Corgi/Bantam Books,
Cash Sales Department,
P.O. Box 11, Falmouth, Cornwall TR10 9EN

Please send a cheque or postal order (no currency) and allow 8op for postage and packing for the first book plus 20p for each additional book ordered up to a maximum charge of £2.00 in UK.

B.F.P.O. customers please allow 8op for the first book and 20p for each additional book.

Overseas customers, including Eire, please allow £1.50 for postage and packing for the first book, £1.00 for the second book, and 30p for each subsequent title ordered.

NAME (Block Letters) ....

ADDRESS ....

....